W9-DCH-911

"You'll sign a paper," Laura said.

"Paper?" Shane echoed.

"Agreeing not to expect me to—well, we'll have separate bedrooms and such."

He watched her blush. "You can be sure I'll never approach you in that way." He paused. "Unless you want me to."

"Never!" burst from her lips.

"I'll sign the paper," Shane said hastily.

What were they doing, the two of them? Something neither wanted, that was for sure. But Shane would do anything to keep custody of his little sister, and Laura, thankfully, had agreed. So here he was, marrying a perfect stranger, and the deal wasn't going to be as easy as he'd assumed....

Dear Reader,

Happy anniversary! Twenty years ago, in May, 1980, we launched Silhouette Books. Much has changed since then, but our gratitude to you, our many readers, and our dedication to bringing you the best that romance fiction has to offer, remains as true today as it did in 1980. Thank you for sharing with us the joy of romance, and for looking toward a wonderful future with us. The best is yet to come!

Those winsome mavericks are back with brand-new stories to tell beneath the Big Sky! *The Kincaid Bride* by Jackie Merritt marks the launch of the MONTANA MAVERICKS: WED IN WHITEHORN series, which focuses on a new generation of Kincaids. This heartwarming marriage-of-convenience tale leads into Silhouette's exciting twelve-book continuity.

Romance is in the air in *The Millionaire She Married,* a continuation of the popular CONVENIENTLY YOURS miniseries by reader favorite Christine Rimmer. And searing passion unites a fierce Native American hero with his stunning soul mate in *Warrior's Embrace* by Peggy Webb.

If you enjoy romantic odysseys, journey to exotic El Bahar in *The Sheik's Arranged Marriage* by Susan Mallery—book two in the sizzling DESERT ROGUES miniseries.

Gail Link pulls heartstrings with her tender tale about a secret child who brings two lovebirds together in *Sullivan's Child.* And to cap off the month, you'll adore *Wild Mustang* by Jane Toombs—a riveting story about a raven-haired horse wrangler who sweeps a breathtaking beauty off her feet.

It's a spectacular month of reading in Special Edition. Enjoy!

All the best,

Karen Taylor Richman
Senior Editor

Please address questions and book requests to:
Silhouette Reader Service
U.S.: 3010 Walden Ave., P.O. Box 1325, Buffalo, NY 14269
Canadian: P.O. Box 609, Fort Erie, Ont. L2A 5X3

JANE TOOMBS
WILD MUSTANG

SPECIAL EDITION®

Published by Silhouette Books
America's Publisher of Contemporary Romance

If you purchased this book without a cover you should be aware that this book is stolen property. It was reported as "unsold and destroyed" to the publisher, and neither the author nor the publisher has received any payment for this "stripped book."

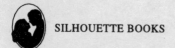 SILHOUETTE BOOKS

ISBN 0-373-24326-X

WILD MUSTANG

Copyright © 2000 by Jane Toombs

All rights reserved. Except for use in any review, the reproduction or utilization of this work in whole or in part in any form by any electronic, mechanical or other means, now known or hereafter invented, including xerography, photocopying and recording, or in any information storage or retrieval system, is forbidden without the written permission of the editorial office, Silhouette Books, 300 East 42nd Street, New York, NY 10017 U.S.A.

All characters in this book have no existence outside the imagination of the author and have no relation whatsoever to anyone bearing the same name or names. They are not even distantly inspired by any individual known or unknown to the author, and all incidents are pure invention.

This edition published by arrangement with Harlequin Books S.A.

® and TM are trademarks of Harlequin Books S.A., used under license. Trademarks indicated with ® are registered in the United States Patent and Trademark Office, the Canadian Trade Marks Office and in other countries.

Visit Silhouette at www.eHarlequin.com

Printed in U.S.A.

Books by Jane Toombs

Silhouette Special Edition

Nobody's Baby #1081
Baby of Mine #1182
Accidental Parents #1247
Designated Daddy #1271
Wild Mustang #1326

Silhouette Shadows

Return to Bloodstone House #5
Dark Enchantment #12
What Waits Below #16
The Volan Curse #35
The Woman in White #50
The Abandoned Bride #56

Previously published under the pseudonym Diana Stuart

Silhouette Special Edition

Out of a Dream #353
The Moon Pool #671

Silhouette Desire

Prime Specimen #172
Leader of the Pack #238
The Shadow Between #257

JANE TOOMBS

was born in California, raised in the upper peninsula of
Michigan and has moved from New York to Nevada as
a result of falling in love with the state and a Nevadan.
Jane has five children, two stepchildren and seven
grandchildren. Her interests include gardening, reading
and knitting.

IT'S OUR 20th ANNIVERSARY!
We'll be celebrating all year,
Continuing with these fabulous titles,
On sale in May 2000.

Romance

 #1444 Mercenary's Woman
Diana Palmer

#1445 Too Hard To Handle
Rita Rainville

 #1446 A Royal Mission
Elizabeth August

#1447 Tall, Strong & Cool Under Fire
Marie Ferrarella

 #1448 Hannah Gets a Husband
Julianna Morris

#1449 Her Sister's Child
Lilian Darcy

Desire

 #1291 Dr. Irresistible
Elizabeth Bevarly

 #1292 Expecting His Child
Leanne Banks

#1293 In His Loving Arms
Cindy Gerard

 #1294 Sheikh's Honor
Alexandra Sellers

#1295 The Baby Bonus
Metsy Hingle

#1296 Did You Say Married?!
Kathie DeNosky

Intimate Moments

 #1003 Rogue's Reform
Marilyn Pappano

 #1004 The Cowboy's Hidden Agenda
Kathleen Creighton

#1005 In a Heartbeat
Carla Cassidy

 #1006 Anything for Her Marriage
Karen Templeton

#1007 Every Little Thing
Linda Winstead Jones

 #1008 Remember the Night
Linda Castillo

Special Edition

#1321 The Kincaid Bride
Jackie Merritt

 #1322 The Millionaire She Married
Christine Rimmer

#1323 Warrior's Embrace
Peggy Webb

#1324 The Sheik's Arranged Marriage
Susan Mallery

#1325 Sullivan's Child
Gail Link

#1326 Wild Mustang
Jane Toombs

Chapter One

The narrow and sparsely traveled blacktopped road leading to the Paiute reservation was in need of repair. There were no fences and, to either side, Nevada's high desert rolled away in acres of silvery sagebrush and other native plants and grasses. Through the open windows of her rental car, Laura Walker breathed in the sage-tinged spring air, keeping tabs on the wild mustang herd to her left.

As usual, one of the mares was in the lead, the black stallion in rearguard position, protecting his harem. While Laura watched, the lead mare—a dun—altered course, obviously heading for the road. Laura pulled the car to the shoulder and stopped, not wanting to miss seeing the wild horses close-up.

As they neared the road, she counted five mares,

the stallion, two yearlings, and one foal, doing its best to keep up. Two mares, one a pinto, one a chestnut, looked to be pregnant and, if she wasn't mistaken, the spotted mare, now lagging behind the stallion, was lame. The rest of the herd seemed healthy.

The lead mare crossed directly in front of the parked car, the other mustangs following her. Laura caught her breath in admiration of their grace and beauty.

Last was the spotted mare who, Laura now saw, definitely limped. The lame mare was almost across the road when a green pickup zoomed into sight, boom box throbbing. Without slowing, the truck roared past. The startled mare lurched ahead, colliding with the foal and knocking it off its feet.

When Laura saw the baby horse was having trouble getting back up, she flung herself from the car and dashed across the road to try to help. Was the foal injured? She hoped it was nothing serious.

Her attention fixed on the foal, Laura paid no attention to the other mustangs who'd gone on ahead. She hadn't quite reached the foal when it managed to struggle to its feet unaided, so she stopped, resisting the impulse to touch the baby. She wasn't here to interfere.

A high-pitched angry scream from behind her made her whirl. Horrified, she stared at the charging, black stallion. He must have decided she was a threat to his harem and circled back without her noticing. Fear froze her—he'd cut her off from her car, and there was no other safe place in sight.

Hooves thrummed from behind her. Before she could move, she found herself grabbed, hoisted into the air, and deposited facedown across a rider's lap like a sack of potatoes, whooshing the breath from her lungs.

As he urged his gray gelding away from the mustangs, Shane Bearclaw kicked him into a gallop to get away from the roused stallion as fast as possible.

"Stupid," he muttered, meaning it for the blond woman he'd rescued. "Could've been killed."

When he reached the rise where he'd been when he first noticed her get out of her car, he reined in Cloud and looked to see if the black stallion had calmed down. The herd was moving off, away from the rise. Reaching down, he pulled up the blonde, so she more or less sat on his lap.

"You figure this was a good day to die?" he growled.

She stared at him from frightened eyes as blue as Lake Tahoe, holding her body stiffly away from him. Serve her right to be scared. She'd sure as hell scared the devil out of him.

"The mustangs are *wild,* and the word means what it says," he told her. "Wild stallions are dangerous. Anybody with sense doesn't go near them."

"Let me down." Her voice quavered so badly he had trouble making out her words.

"Not unless you promise to get up behind me until I get you to your car. I have no intention of trusting you until I see you get in and drive away.

My rodeo days are long gone—I'm not up to trying that trick twice in one day.''

He found himself wishing those spectacular blue eyes didn't look so fearful. "Hey, it's over," he said, in softer tones, suddenly aware that no matter how foolish she might have been, he was holding a very pretty blonde on his lap.

"I'm Shane Bearclaw," he said, realizing he wanted to know who she was.

Laura looked into the dark eyes of this stranger who held her far too close to him. His long black hair was tied back, revealing a strong-featured face. In a way, he reminded her of the stallion who'd threatened her. She found Shane Bearclaw equally threatening.

"Laura Walker," she managed to say. "I was coming to meet you at your ranch. And, yes, I'd much prefer to be seated behind you."

This was not the greatest of beginnings as far as she was concerned. Her fear of him was beginning to abate, leaving in its place an edgy awareness of him as a man. That, she could do without.

He offered a one-sided grin as he slid off the gray. "So you're the semi-Fed in person."

"The what?" she asked as she eased back until she was behind the saddle.

He remounted. "Anyone who arrives on the reservation with the Fed's blessing."

"I have a federal grant, but I'm not otherwise connected in any way with the government." Indignation threaded through her words.

A shrug told her that he intended to go on thinking of her as he darn well pleased. Deciding she'd delayed far too long in demanding to be taken back to her car, she remedied that in crisp tones.

"If you'll drop me off at my car, I'll meet you at your ranch, and we can then discuss how I can best meet my objectives with your help."

Without a word, he urged his horse into motion, and she found holding onto him was almost as intimate as sitting on his lap. But it was either hang on or fall off.

What seemed like long minutes later, he halted the gray by her car, slid off, and helped her down. "How good are your directions?" he asked. "The ranch isn't on a main road."

"Sketchy," she admitted, stepping away from him.

He rattled off his own version of how to get there.

She nodded and got into the car. Watching him ride away, she realized he was a superb horseman and belatedly remembered that she'd forgotten to thank him for rescuing her. No wonder. No sooner had she gotten her breath back from being suddenly flung onto a horse, when she'd found herself sitting on a strange man's lap.

Laura had thought her uneasiness around men was under control, but she hadn't anticipated such an intimate confrontation as she'd had with Shane Bearclaw. And this was the man she'd be working with over the next month or so. A take-charge macho-type who wouldn't equate brains with women.

Learn to reserve judgment. Laura could almost hear her therapist's voice. *Men are not all the same.*

Maybe not. Maybe that big brute on the horse hadn't been trying to intimidate her. But it certainly felt that way.

"Tenderfoot," Shane muttered to himself as he rode back to the ranch. Laura Walker, slim and fragile-looking, didn't strike him as a woman who'd be a happy camper out on the range.

He'd cooperate as promised, but he hoped her mustang studies, whatever they were, wouldn't take long. He had enough problems without shepherding a greenhorn around—the major one being his fear of losing his custody battle.

"You know I prefer leaving a child in the home she's accustomed to," Judge Rankin had told him last week. "But, face it, Shane, there's no woman in your household. The child's father has remarried and he and his wife offer a stable environment for the little girl."

"The ranch is a good environment," Shane had protested, deliberately misunderstanding.

Judge Rankin had given him a level look. "If you were married, I'd have no problem."

Shane pressed the gelding into a lope. Married? Not a hope. Not ever again. He'd sworn off it.

After driving along several unmarked gravel roads, Laura pulled into the small oasis surrounding the Bearclaw ranch house. Her brother had told her the desert soil was fertile, all it needed was water and anything would grow. The greenery around the house proved him right. Besides the flowering shrubs near the house foundation, massive cotton-woods shaded the long, low building, testifying to how long people had lived in this spot.

As she left the car, she saw the neat green rows of a fenced-in vegetable garden. Otherwise the yard was left as the desert intended, with no lawn for water to be wasted on. Outbuildings in back included a barn with an attached corral. The house itself was adobe brick with a tile roof.

Before she reached the front door, it opened and a dark-haired girl of about nine or ten stood framed in the doorway. Unlike Shane, she had hazel eyes.

"Hi," she said, "I'm Sage. You must be Ms. Walker. Shane said you were coming today, and I've been waiting. Grandfather has, too, but he doesn't get antsy like me. You're lots prettier than I thought you'd be."

Shane's daughter? Laura smiled at her. "Then I guess you couldn't have expected very much."

"Please come in," Sage said, stepping aside so Laura could enter.

Ushered into a pleasantly uncluttered living room, Laura chose an attractively decorated leather chair to sit in.

"I made iced tea," Sage told her. "Would you like some? It's real tea, not out of a jar 'cause Grandfather hates instant stuff."

"Thank you, I would," Laura told her, touched by the little girl's effort to be a good hostess.

It then occurred to her that the child might actually be the only hostess in the house. She hadn't mentioned a mother, only a grandfather.

A carving of a horse—surely a wild mustang—on the mantel of the stone fireplace caught Laura's eye. She rose to take a closer look and was admiring how well the carver seemed to have captured the mustang spirit when Sage came back with a tray.

"This horse is beautiful," she told the girl.

Sage nodded. "Shane says he senses what animal is in the wood before he starts carving. Grandfather says that's the mark of a medicine man. So now Shane's learning all that medicine stuff."

She set the tray carefully on a polished slab of wood masquerading as a coffee table and offered a paper napkin and a glass to Laura. "Do you take sugar or sweetener?" she asked. "'Cause I didn't put any in, in case you don't."

"This is how I like my tea," Laura said, resuming her seat, trying to integrate the scowling man who'd rescued her with the obviously sensitive sculptor.

"I like lots of sugar," Sage confided. "So does Grandfather."

As if that was a cue, a gray-haired older man, still ramrod straight, entered the room. His hair, like Shane's, was long and tied back. His shrewd, dark eyes fixed on Laura.

"Grandfather," Sage said, "this is Ms. Walker."

The old man nodded. "Howell Bearclaw," he

told her. "I don't like being called mister, and I don't like being called Howell much, either. I prefer Grandfather. To us, that's a title of respect." Unexpectedly, he grinned at her.

"You don't have to call me that till you find something about me to respect. What'll we call you?"

She smiled. "I like being called Laura."

Sage handed him a glass of tea. He tasted it, nodded in approval, and took the chair opposite Laura's.

"You've come to count the wild horses on our land," he said.

She shook her head. "Not exactly. My government grant is for determining the overall health of the mustang herds. Nevada, and your reservation, is my first stop. Later, I'll be doing the same thing in the other states where they range. The Bureau of Land Management estimates Nevada has 22,500 of the 42,000 wild horses in the West."

He grunted. "At least you don't call them estrays like the BLM. What kind of word is that? Wild is wild."

Recalling the stallion, Laura had to agree. Government agencies like the BLM had their own names for things, but wild was most certainly wild.

"My grandson's going to ride out with you," he said.

Though it wasn't a question, Laura nodded. "I hope he doesn't mind." Thinking about her meeting with Shane, she was none too sure he was happy about it.

"He's no grandson of mine if he doesn't jump at the chance to escort a pretty woman," Grandfather said.

"I already told her she was pretty," Sage put in. "She's nice, too."

"Must be smart, too, to get that grant."

Laura was somewhat taken aback at the turn of conversation—almost as though she weren't there.

Sage turned to her and asked, "Are you married?"

Since there was no reason not to answer, Laura replied, "No, I'm not." She didn't add that she never would be, either. That was none of their business.

Sage and her grandfather exchanged a look.

What on earth is all this about? Laura asked herself.

"That makes three of us," Grandfather said.

Sage giggled. "I'm too young to be married."

Grandfather frowned at her. "And I suppose you figure I'm too old."

They both gazed at Laura. What did they expect her to say? Like Goldilocks, that her age was just right?

"Marriage isn't on my agenda," she said flatly.

"We are not behaving like proper hosts," Grandfather said. "We've embarrassed our guest by asking a personal question."

"I'm sorry," Sage said. "It's just that Laura's so pretty I thought she must be married."

They were at it again, talking about her as if she

weren't in the same room. Though she was inclined to like both of them, she found this trait disturbing. She doubted it was a Paiute custom.

"We are alone too much, Laura," Grandfather said, this time addressing her directly.

"Yes," Sage chimed in. "So will you forgive us?"

"I wasn't offended," she assured them.

"He's coming," Grandfather said. "I'll go out and take care of Cloud." Looking at Sage, he added, "You stay and entertain our guest." He left the room.

Though Laura presumed he meant Shane, she hadn't heard anything to indicate Shane's immediate arrival.

"You didn't ask me what grade I'm in and where I go to school," Sage told her.

"Should I have?"

Sage shook her head. "Most people do. It gets boring 'cause they don't really care. Grandfather says never ask a question unless you really want to hear the answer. But then it usually turns out that the questions you want to ask are personal, and people don't want to answer them."

Laura took this as a roundabout apology. "Yes, that's a real bummer, isn't it?"

She was rewarded with a brilliant smile. "As soon as I heard you were coming, I knew I was going to like you," Sage said.

"I didn't know you existed until I got here, but now that we've met, I hope we'll get to know one another better."

"Yeah. Me, too." Sage raised her head as though listening. "Here comes Shane." She gazed expectantly at the entrance to the living room.

Only then did Laura hear booted footsteps.

"Excuse me, I have to talk to Grandfather," Sage said, rising and darting from the room.

Leaving me to face the ogre alone, Laura thought, setting down her empty glass.

In walked Shane, even more impressively masculine than Laura had remembered—stiffening her resolve not to let him intimidate her. Attractive, yes, but that didn't make him any more appealing to her.

Shane eyed Laura, sitting up straight with her feet crossed ladylike at the ankles, her dressy pantsuit neat, despite the untidy rescue. A city girl. He groaned inwardly, knowing he was stuck with her for at least a month, maybe more. Yeah, she was pretty in her own quiet way, but that wouldn't make his nursemaid task any easier.

"I was remiss in not immediately thanking you for rescuing me," Laura said primly.

The way she said it made him feel she didn't like him any the better for saving her life.

"We're both lucky it worked," he said bluntly.

Laura nodded, wishing he'd sit down. It made her nervous to be loomed over.

"Shall we discuss what kind of a schedule would best suit you?" she asked. "I'm quite flexible."

"Let's make sure I know what you want from me."

"I'd like to borrow a horse to ride, if that's possible,'' she said. At his nod, she continued. ''Since this is your home territory, I hope you'll be able to locate the herds on the reservation for me so I can count the horses and get an overall impression of their health.''

''First—you *do* understand that mustangs make no distinction between reservation land, BLM land, or privately owned ranch land? They aren't 'our' horses, they're free-ranging.''

''I'm quite aware of that, but I understand at least two herds seem to spend most of their time on Paiute land.'' Laura was congratulating herself on her businesslike approach despite her nervousness, when Sage popped into the room.

''Grandfather has asked me to invite you to stay here at the ranch with us,'' Sage said to Laura. ''Please say you will. We have lots of room, and it'll be way more convenient for you. Otherwise, you'll have to drive back and forth from Reno all the time.''

Though taken aback, Laura noticed Shane seemed even more surprised than she was at the invitation.

Before Laura could respond, Sage added plaintively, ''I really wish you'd stay here, so we could get to know each other better, like you said.''

Sympathy for Sage's need for female company shot down Laura's instinctive refusal before the words passed her lips. She understood what it was to be lonely.

Shane frowned at Sage. ''I don't think Ms. Walker would want to—''

Laura cut him off. ''Please tell your grandfather

I'm grateful for his thoughtfulness," she said to the girl. "If Mr. Bearclaw here approves, I accept the kind offer."

Privately, she reserved her right to retreat to a Reno hotel if it proved uncomfortable to be in the same house with Shane.

"Stay, by all means," Shane said, in such a determinedly neutral tone, that Laura knew he'd been hoping she'd refuse.

Maybe that was part of the reason she'd accepted. Certainly if *he'd* invited her, she never would have, though the truth was, staying at the ranch would be more convenient.

"I'll bring my things with me when I come in the morning, then," Laura said. Looking at Shane, she added, "What time will you be ready to ride?"

He raised an eyebrow. "Whenever you get here."

Since Sage was so eager to play hostess, Shane let her show Laura to the door, watching her walk away despite not meaning to. She moved as gracefully as any mare, which was, coming from him, a compliment. So many women either plodded or sashayed, neither of which conveyed grace.

Without willing himself to, he wandered to the window where he'd be able to see her get into her car.

"Laura will be good company for Sage while she's here," Grandfather said from in back of him, having arrived soundlessly, as usual. "That's why I told Sage to ask her to stay with us."

Shane turned to face him. "I wondered why you hadn't bothered to consult me."

"Partners in running the ranch we may be, but I am still Grandfather."

"Yes, Respected Elder." Shane said the words with affectionate mockery.

Grandfather grinned at him. "And don't you forget it."

Shane had to agree that female company would be good for Sage, but he'd be willing to bet old Bearclaw had something else up his sleeve. Grandfather had the most devious mind on the res. And more than likely in the entire state of Nevada.

Still, what could be his scheme? He'd never interfered in Shane's private life, so the fact Laura was a woman shouldn't have anything to do with it, other than her being company for Sage, like he'd said. What then? The mustangs? The fact that she might have some sort of in with the Feds?

Shane shook his head to both possibilities. Maybe he was just imagining Grandfather planning something. What would be the point?

Chapter Two

As Laura drove back from the reservation to Reno, she told herself she shouldn't have been swayed, by her empathy with Sage, into accepting the invitation to stay at the Bearclaw ranch. She was bound to be uncomfortable in Shane's house. It would be difficult enough when they rode together in search of the wild horses—why had she let herself in for more awkwardness in the evenings?

Though she didn't trust *any* man except her brother Nathan, Shane was typical of the kind of man who unnerved her the most. He was big and rugged and so very much *there*. If he was present, he couldn't be ignored.

Yet, how could she have resisted the appeal in Sage's eyes? The girl so obviously wanted her to agree to stay. What had happened to the girl's mother? she wondered. Laura had gotten the distinct feeling there was no woman in the Bearclaw home.

She really hadn't minded the girl's personal questions because she felt they were innocent, that Sage merely wanted to know more about her. In any case, the girl hadn't been the first one to ask Laura if she was married. Sometimes people went on to ask why not, which was far more offensive. The first question was easy to answer. The second was not, and she didn't even try, but merely shrugged and either walked away or changed the subject.

The truth was, despite the therapy Laura had been through over the years, she'd never been able to convince herself that kind words and smiles from men weren't a cover for deception of some kind. The best protection was to stay single. Permanently.

At the hotel, she was reluctant to go to her room after she ate because there was nothing to do there except watch TV. So she wandered through the casino, eyeing the devotees at the slot machines, but not venturing even a nickel of her own money.

There is such a thing as being over-cautious. Her therapist's words. Laura shrugged. Maybe she was, but caution kept her safe, didn't it?

As usual, she ignored the occasional male stares and comments aimed at any, even minimally attractive, unaccompanied young woman. She'd gotten so effective at this, very few men ever persisted in coming on to her. Pausing to listen to the trio in the lounge for a time, she admired the female singer's performance, as the woman swayed and gestured in time to the music. True, it was no more than a performance, but a tinge of envy made Laura sigh. The singer seemed so naturally uninhibited that she was a pleasure to watch.

If only I could act even half that free and easy, Laura thought. If only I didn't have to keep monitoring my behavior so I don't attract attention from men.

Finally feeling the effects of jet lag, she went to her room and got ready for bed. Though she fell asleep right away, she kept rousing throughout the night, probably because she was so apprehensive about working with Shane. Near dawn she finally got up, dressed in riding jeans, boots, and Western shirt and went down to eat breakfast. One great advantage of Nevada casino-hotels was being able to eat at any hour of the day or night. Twenty-four-hour service. Breakfast over, she decided to head for the ranch, even though she'd be arriving really early. It'd serve macho Shane right if she got there before he was up. Quickly packing her belongings, she checked out.

When she got to the ranch house, Sage answered her knock and insisted on helping to carry in her things.

"Grandfather and Shane are in the barn," Sage said, when Laura was settled into a sparsely furnished but comfortable-looking bedroom. "There's coffee if you want some."

After refusing any food, Laura sat in the kitchen with Sage, drinking a mug of coffee.

"Whoa," the girl said. "For somebody who doesn't put anything in tea, you sure use a lot of sugar in your coffee. And cream, too."

Laura grinned at her. "It goes to show no one's perfect, not even me."

"I guess." Sage fidgeted in her chair, finally adding, "I'm not supposed to ask any personal stuff, but I might forget. You won't get mad, will you?"

After shaking her head, Laura said, "I think maybe it's my turn to ask questions."

"Cool. I don't care if they're personal ones." Sage looked at her expectantly.

After discovering who the girl's favorite actors and singers were, Laura asked about her friends.

"Maria and Donna are my two best friends," Sage told her. "They live on the res, too, but not very nearby. Sometimes I mind we can't get together oftener, but mostly I don't. I'm sort of used to hanging out with Grandfather." She hesitated, and then said vehemently, "I don't ever want to move away from here. Never ever. If they try to make me move to smoggy L.A., I won't go."

"Are Shane and your grandfather planning to move there?"

Sage shook her head. "It's my father. He got married again, and now he wants me to come and live with him and her. I don't even know her."

Laura blinked. Up until now, she'd assumed Sage was Shane's daughter.

Looking down at the table where she traced spirals with her finger, Sage said, "Me and my mom left him when I was four 'cause he was mean to her. We came here to live with my brother Shane and Grandfather. Then she got sick and died two years ago. Shane told me I could stay at the ranch forever if I wanted. Now my father is trying to make the judge say I have to leave and go live with him." She blinked back tears.

Laura scooted her chair over and put an arm around the girl's shoulders.

"I'm scared," Sage confessed. "I don't remember my father too good. What if he's still mean? I don't want to leave Shane and Grandfather, but what if the judge makes me? Why don't I get to say what *I* want?"

Her heart touched, Laura hugged the girl closer. It sickened her to think that Sage might ever become the victim of an abusive father. She wished she could promise the girl that she'd be able to choose where she wanted to live. Impossible, when she knew nothing about the circumstances.

The kitchen door opened, and Sage pulled away. Laura stood up and faced Shane, feeling a shock at the reality of him. When he wasn't present, it was easier to categorize him and pretend to herself she'd be able to deal with him. Up close, she found him overwhelming.

"Good," he told her, his gaze flicking over her, no doubt assessing how appropriate her clothes were for riding. "We can get an early start. Hope you brought a broad-brimmed hat—at this altitude, you'll need one to prevent sunburn.''

Despite telling herself she intended to limit her reply to a curt nod, she found herself saying, ''I've been in this part of Nevada before. Naturally I brought a hat. And sunscreen.''

He was the one who gave the curt nod. ''Let's get going then.''

Sage trailed them to the corral and shook her head over the mare Shane had chosen for Laura. ''Rabbit's for scaredy-cat beginners,'' she told her brother. ''I bet you never even asked Laura what kind of a rider she was.''

Laura smiled to herself. Of course he hadn't, being one of those men who knew best. She waited, determined not to say anything until he spoke.

''The question isn't how good you are,'' he said to Laura, ''but how long a ride you're accustomed to.''

''I qualify somewhere above a scaredy-cat beginner,'' she said coolly, making herself stare into those dark, fathomless eyes.

He shrugged and turned to his sister. ''I suppose you want to do the picking.''

''I sure can do better than Rabbit,'' Sage told him. ''How about Columbine?'' She pointed to what looked to Laura like an Arabian mare, a chestnut. ''That's her name but we call her Colly.''

Shane raised his eyebrows at Laura.

''Colly's beautiful,'' she said. ''I'd like to ride her. Arabian, isn't she?''

He smiled. "Some of her ancestry must have been, but she's of mustang stock. We picked her up as a filly who'd been injured. By the time she was healthy and whole, she was too domesticated to turn loose, so we kept her. On the trail, Colly can outlast any horse we own." His dubious glance told her he didn't think she'd come anywhere close to Colly's ability.

After Cloud and Colly were saddled, Shane and Laura set off, with Sage waving from the corral.

"I hope we'll be able to spot the black stallion's herd again," Laura said after they'd ridden some time in silence. "One of his mares—a pregnant pinto—was lame. I need to get a better look at her."

"He's got two pinto mares. Which one?" Shane's words made her certain he must know every mustang in that herd.

"If she were a cat I'd call her a calico."

He nodded. "I know the one. Must be a recent injury. She wasn't lame the last time I got a good look at the herd."

"It was obvious yesterday." As soon as the words were out she realized he probably hadn't noticed the mare, being too busy coming to her rescue. The sooner she came to terms with that the better.

"Yesterday wasn't the greatest introduction in the world for us," she said, facing her mistake squarely. "It was poor judgment for me not to pay closer attention to the stallion."

Shane had been wondering if she'd ever admit her mistake. Now that she had, he was forced to revise his estimate of her. She also sat on Colly like a pro and rode well. The question that remained was how long she could last.

She was quiet for some time before saying, "This morning Sage told me something that keeps troubling me. Is it true her father is trying to gain custody? She seems terrified that he will."

The last thing Shane wanted to do was discuss his problems with a stranger, but since his sister had already hung out the family laundry, the least he could do would be to give Laura the straight facts.

"My mother had me when she was very young. My father died when I was eighteen, and two years later, she remarried off the reservation and went to live with her husband in southern California. Sage was born there. My mother brought her back to the ranch when she was four, and the two of them never left."

"Sage said her father was mean," Laura said.

"Our mother told us that," Shane said shortly, a muscle tightening in his jaw. From the moment his mother had come home, he'd hated Bill Jennings, the man who'd become his stepfather.

Just as quickly, he'd come to love his little sister. The thought of Sage going to live with that man set his teeth on edge.

"Surely no judge would force a child to live with a man known to be abusive," Laura said, her indignation clear in her voice.

"There's no evidence of any abuse. When she lived with him, my mother never called the authorities, so there's no record. And now she's dead. The judge feels since Sage's father has remarried, she'd benefit by having a woman to mother her.''

Laura didn't speak for a while. ''Forgive me if I'm getting too personal,'' she said at last. ''I can't help but be concerned about Sage's future. If the judge seems to think Sage needs a woman's influence, isn't there someone you know that you could marry? Surely the judge wouldn't favor moving Sage then.''

He scowled. ''Marriage is out. It's not for me.''

To his surprise, she nodded. ''I understand because I never intend to marry myself. Still, you might come to some kind of accommodation—I suppose it might be called a marriage in name only— to satisfy the judge. Once he rules in your favor, after a time the marriage could be dissolved.''

He started to brush off the suggestion with a terse remark, then held, staring at her. What was it Grandfather had said last night? Something about what a nice young lady Laura was, just the person Sage needed to have around.

At the time he'd thought Grandfather meant for temporary company. Ha. What that clever old trickster was trying to do was set him up. That was the reason behind his inviting Laura to stay at the ranch.

Shane snorted in disgust at being taken in. Realizing he'd startled Laura, he turned away. She'd had no part in this, he felt almost sure. Not once had she indicated she so much as liked him. He wondered why.

Most women found him attractive. He'd be a fool if he hadn't noticed that. But it was clear to him that Laura didn't. He glanced at her and caught her looking at him apprehensively. Was she afraid of him? Why should she be?

"Is something bothering you?" she said, flinging her words at him like bullets.

He blinked. "What makes you ask?"

"You keep scowling."

Shane hadn't realized he was. "It's not aimed at you." He paused for a moment, then asked, "Why is it you never intend to marry?"

"I—well, I—" she faltered. He watched her take a deep breath and raise her chin. "Due to something that happened in the past, I don't trust men," she went on. "I prefer to have nothing but impersonal dealings with them. I absolutely can't imagine marrying." She gave him a level look. "Why don't *you* intend to marry?"

It wasn't any of her damn business. But, after a moment, he realized he'd posed the question first, and she'd given him an answer. Fair was fair. He owed her some kind of an explanation.

"The usual," he said tersely. "We were young and ignorant, she got pregnant, so we got married. A mistake. We didn't mesh. I took off and joined the rodeo circuit, wasn't home much. She and my daughter were killed in an accident while I was gone." He made a slashing motion with his hand. "Never again."

He had no intention of telling her how Deena had

begun running around and that the fatal accident had
been when she was coming home from her newest
lover's place, the baby with her. Nor was he going
to confess his guilt. If he hadn't run off, if he'd faced
their incompatibility head-on and filed for divorce,
asking for custody of his daughter, both she and
Deena would be alive today.

Hating to hash over the unchangeable past, he
shucked it off by taking a quick look around. Spotting some dust rising, he pointed. "Might be a herd
over that way. We'll head for the nearest rise and
see what it is."

When they paused at the crest of the hill, he saw
he was right, but the mustangs were heading away
from them and were already so far away they'd
never catch up. Any pursuit would simply make
them run all the faster and farther.

"To get close to a herd, you really need to camp
out near a source of water so they'll come to you,"
he said. "Since they normally range over about
twenty acres per day, it's futile to chase them.
That'll just result in them taking off and likely moving off reservation land."

"I can see that," she said. "Shall we plan to
camp tomorrow?" Concealing his surprise that she
didn't balk at camping with him, he said, "Up to
you. But it'll have to wait for a couple of days."

"Whenever you have the time, then." She hesitated before saying, "I want to tell you I'm sorry
about what happened to your wife and child. I re-

alize the tragedy must make it doubly distressing for you now that you have to worry about losing Sage.''

He couldn't lose Sage, that's all there was to it. His sister belonged here, where their mother had brought her, knowing he'd keep the girl safe.

Back at the ranch, Shane found the evening meal livelier with Laura present. Not that she did much talking. She didn't have a chance with Sage and Grandfather both vying for her attention.

After the meal cleanup, Sage brought out her favorite shirt, which she'd torn on a nail in the barn, to show to Laura.

''I don't know how to fix it without having it look gross,'' Sage told her.

Though he seemed intent on the newspaper he was reading, Shane was acutely aware of Laura sitting across from him on the leather couch with his sister. It'd been a long time since there'd been a woman in this living room in the evening.

''You're right. Any repair stitches would show,'' Laura said. ''But what we could do is cover the stitching with embroidery—a flowering branch could run from one end of the repair job to the other.''

''Embroidery?'' Sage sounded as though even the word was alien to her.

''My grandmother taught me when I was about your age. It's not exactly fun, but it's kind of neat to know how to embroider. I can teach you, if you like.''

"But if I'm just learning, I might spoil my shirt."

"Oh, we'll let you practice on the hem of a pillowcase or something like that. Embroidery isn't all that hard once you get the hang of it. We'll need to buy some special thread and some designs, though—in Reno, I suppose."

Shane lowered the newspaper. "There might be what you need in Grandmother's trunk," he said to Sage. "I seem to remember her trying to teach our mother some kind of fancy sewing."

Sage bounced up from the couch. "Whoa! Really? Can we go look in the trunk now?"

From the corner where he'd seemed to be dozing, Grandfather said, "Our daughter wasn't much for fancy work, but she turned out to be the best dancer on the res. Not much for picking good men, either, but I got to admit she turned out two pretty good kids."

Sage grinned at him. "How come you're always telling me I'm bad, then?"

"It's like Coyote—you got two sides." Grandfather turned to Shane. "All that sewing stuff is in one of the reed baskets Grandmother's mother made."

Shane rose and left the room, with Sage trailing him.

"He's a sound man," Grandfather said to Laura. "Once he learns to laugh again, he'll be hard to beat."

Laura tried to think how to respond to this but gave up. She found herself at ease with Grandfather as a man, but she wasn't always sure exactly what he meant.

Reverting to what he'd said to Sage, she asked, "What did you mean about Coyote having two sides?"

"One to do good for the people, the other to play tricks on them. I figure we're all more or less like that." He leaned forward in his chair, fixing her with an intent gaze. "We can't lose Sage. We need her, and she needs us." While Laura believed this to be true, she didn't understand how Grandfather could think she'd be able to help, even though she wanted to.

"So you're going camping with Shane," the old man said, completely changing the subject. At least this one was easy to respond to.

"When he finds time—maybe in a day or two," she said.

Grandfather nodded. "Desert nights."

She was sure his cryptic words meant something that she was missing. "I'm sure they're lovely," she said cautiously.

"Can carry a chill this time of the year," he told her.

That seemed fairly straightforward, but before she could reply, Shane reappeared with Sage who was carrying a beautifully woven, round basket, its muted-colored design scarcely faded with age. The girl dumped the contents of the basket onto the coffee-table, and Laura leaned forward to sort through them. In no time at all, she'd located what she needed and, sooner than Shane would have believed possible, his sister was getting her first lesson in embroidery and, by all indications, having fun.

Grandfather rose and, in passing Shane's chair, murmured, "Get along well, don't they?"

Shane grunted, well aware now of the old man's motives. Grandfather knew very well why Shane would never marry again. He also ought to have known that dangling Laura in front of him, like a carrot held out to entice a mule, was not going to work.

"What you need is a kick in the rear," was Grandfather's parting shot before exiting.

Despite himself, Shane carried to bed with him the image of the two heads—blond and black—bent over the sewing. He had to admit Laura really seemed to like his sister. As for Sage, she was obviously in the throes of heroine worship.

When he woke around three, he found himself weighing the pros and cons of Laura's suggestion about—how had she put it?—a marriage of accommodation. He cast his mind over possible candidates among the women he knew, assessed them and, one by one, rejected them.

Cursing himself for even considering the idea, he turned over and tried to chase down sleep. But as fast as he reached for it, the faster it drew away.

Keep my little girl safe. He heard the echo of his mother's words in his head. She'd known she was dying and hadn't seemed frightened for herself, only for Sage. How easy it had seemed then to think he always would be able to protect his baby sister.

There must be a way. Unfortunately, the only idea he could think of that seemed likely to work had come from Laura, and that one was impossible. There might be more than one woman in the world he'd like to take to bed, but there wasn't any he wanted to marry.

Marriage was a trap. A snare and a delusion. It brought grief and heartache and guilt. And in his mother's case, disillusion and pain. He wanted no part of it.

Chapter Three

Laura was in good spirits as she and Shane rode out early in the cool of the morning. So far, there'd been no problem staying at the ranch. She welcomed the chance to make friends with Sage, although she'd never imagined she'd wind up teaching any girl to embroider.

It was a skill she hadn't called up in years, but, as it turned out, she hadn't forgotten. "Like riding a bicycle," she said aloud.

Shane turned to look at her. "Bicycle?"

"I was thinking that we rarely forget skills we learned as children," she told him.

"I was six when my father taught me how to whittle," he said.

"I admire the mustang on your mantel. You're

really talented. I didn't notice any other pieces, though.''

''Most of what I make goes to the shops to be sold. Keeps us eating.''

If the wild horse was any example, she thought his carvings ought to fetch top prices.

They rode in silence for a while, Laura enjoying the clean desert air and the sight of the snow-capped Sierra peaks in the distance. ''What's the altitude here?'' she asked.

''Over four thousand feet.'' His glance was assessing. ''Tends to bother people coming from near sea level.''

''So if I sleep in, that's why?'' she asked. Actually she'd had trouble forcing herself out of bed this morning. Sheer determination had fueled her I'll-show-him attitude or she'd still be asleep.

He half-smiled. ''Somehow, I don't think you will.''

After another silence, he pointed to some sleek, streamlined clouds drifting over the Sierra peaks. ''Lenticulars. Some weather heading our way. You can feel the dampness in the air.''

''You're the local weather expert—I'll take your word for it.''

''Smell the air.''

It was an order, so she did. His raised eyebrows told her that he expected a comment.

''The scent of sage is maybe a bit stronger than usual.''

He nodded. ''Damp air.''

She wondered if she'd passed some kind of test. Not that she cared. No, wait, that wasn't true. She did want to impress upon him that she wasn't a person to be given the slowest, safest mare in the corral. She was a professional who knew what she was doing, and sooner or later he'd be forced to recognize it.

A plume of dust caught her eye. Before she could point it out, he said, "We'll head for those cottonwoods to the right. They run along a stream, and chances are the herd's coming to the water. If we get there first and stay still, we won't spook 'em."

He was right. As they waited under the branches covered with the bright green leaves of early June, the mustangs they'd spotted gathered upstream—five of them. To her disappointment, the calico pinto mare wasn't among them. In fact—weren't they all stallions?

"Is that what they call a bachelor herd?" she asked in a low tone, admiring a white horse a bit smaller than the others.

"Right. All young males who haven't collected a harem yet."

As they watched the mustangs drink, then wheel and trot off, Laura was once again awed by their fluid grace. She'd never imagined she'd be so moved by the sight of wild horses.

"Might as well dismount and take a break," Shane said.

Somewhat surprised, since they hadn't been riding long, she agreed. Once off the mare, she wandered down to the stream—narrow, but containing a respectable amount of water. From what her brother had told her about Nevada, she figured this was snow-melt and that, later in the summer, the creek might run dry.

Dipping her fingers in the cold water confirmed her guess. Rejoining Shane near the trunk of a good-sized tree, she turned up her face for a moment to feel the warmth of the sun filtering through the leafy branches. What a peaceful scene. She'd have relaxed completely if only she hadn't been so aware of the man standing no more that two feet away.

"I've been doing some thinking," he said, not looking at her.

She waited. When he didn't go on, she asked, "About what?"

"About what you said."

She'd said a lot of things. "You'll have to be specific."

Shane flicked her a glance. This was going to be even harder than he'd thought. He sure as hell didn't want to say what must be said or do what must be done. The trouble was, he couldn't figure any other way.

When he'd roused in the grayness of pre-dawn, he'd seen the solution there before him, like jigsaw puzzle pieces fitted together, each piece a separate entity, but together creating a whole. Like a puzzle, it could be taken apart again, which was the only reason he'd considered it.

"It's about my sister," he said. "I didn't tell you

yesterday, but Judge Rankin warned me I ought to get married or else he'd have trouble letting me keep Sage. Then you talked about what you called a marriage of accommodation.''

She smiled at him. ''Yes, I did. I really do think that's your best choice at this point, since you don't seem to have any woman in mind you really want to marry.''

''So you agree.''

He caught her nod from the corner of his eye. Good. This might turn out to be simpler than he'd figured. Still it was hard to get the words out.

''Grandfather seconds my choice,'' he temporized. ''In fact, it was his choice first.''

''All the better.''

Go for it, man, he told himself. Stop hedging. Facing her directly, he said, ''Grandfather thinks you're the perfect person for the judge to accept, and I've decided he's right. Since I don't want to get married and neither do you, we are, as the ads say, made for each other—at least as far as this situation goes.'' He cut off his nervous babbling. Damn, but he was on edge.

She stared up at him, her mouth slightly open. He hadn't before noticed how perfectly shaped her lips were. Not that it mattered. He kept waiting for her to speak, but she seemed dumbstruck.

''Well?'' he muttered.

''I—uh—I—'' She swallowed and stopped, looking as wild-eyed as a frightened mustang.

"What's wrong?" he demanded. "It *was* your idea."

"Well, yes, but I didn't mean me," she sputtered. "I can't—I couldn't possibly. No."

"Why not? It's not like it's for real."

"But you—that is, I—what I mean is, I don't want to expose myself to—" She broke off, looking away from him.

"Expose yourself to what? Me? Hell, I thought you understood I don't want anything from you except your agreement to be a wife on paper."

"I do understand that. But I—"

"You're scared."

"No!"

He laid a hand on her shoulder, removing it before she could flinch away. "Then why are you trembling?" he asked. "You remind me of a spooked mare."

With great effort, Laura pulled herself together. There was no use trying to explain. Shane couldn't possibly understand why she was "spooked."

"I'm sorry," she said stiffly. "I just can't. Shall we get on with our ride?"

They'd made a sweep of one section of the reservation without coming across any mustangs before Shane suggested they start back. Up until then, neither of them had said a word.

"We'll be taking a day off tomorrow," he added. "No point in riding in the rain, and it'll give me a chance to get into town."

Laura had no doubt it would rain. Even she could now feel the change in the air—which corresponded to a change in her. Though she still viewed his proposal askance, she was beginning to ask herself if she hadn't overreacted.

Shane didn't want to get married any more than she did. Surely he'd be amenable to putting everything in writing—separate rooms and all that. Did she believe he'd abide by the written agreement? That was the poser.

Supposing she did believe he would—could she then tolerate the idea of such a marriage?

When they reached the barn, she was still pondering the possibility. Seeing Sage come running out to meet them, her face alight with welcome, Laura's heart contracted. How vulnerable the girl was. Sage must never be allowed to go through anything even vaguely similar to what had happened to her when she was young. Never!

I'll talk to Grandfather, Laura decided. He knows Shane far better than I.

Her chance came almost immediately. Sage had been invited to Donna's house for a sleepover and wanted Shane's permission. When he gave it, she then needed a ride to her friend's house, some distance away.

"I'm sorry I didn't start supper," Sage said to Laura. "I was going to make chicken enchiladas. Donna's mom showed me how, and I wrote it down. It's real easy."

Laura smiled at her. "That's good, because I've never made them. I can cook, though, honest."

"Oh, I knew you could cook. I expect you can do most anything. But this recipe is sort of different 'cause there's no tomatoes in it. You don't mind having to get supper ready?"

Laura shook her head. "Not a bit. You go and enjoy the sleepover with Donna."

"Is it all right if I hug you goodbye?" Sage asked, when she had her sleeping gear piled by the door.

Laura responded by hugging Sage. "Have a good time," she told the girl.

After the door closed behind Shane and his sister, Laura sighed. How long had it been since she'd hugged anyone? Not since she'd last seen her brother and his wife and their son Tim. She hadn't visited them yet on this trip to Nevada because she'd wanted to start working first.

She walked slowly back into the kitchen and found Grandfather seated at the table with a glass of iced tea. "Sage made you some without sugar," he said, nodding his head toward the refrigerator.

After pouring herself a glass, Laura sat down across from him.

"You got the look of someone with a troubled heart," he said.

"It's Sage," she said, approaching the subject at a tangent. "She doesn't want to leave you and Shane and it sounds as though she may have to unless—" She hesitated, uncertain how to go on.

"Unless you marry Shane."

Laura blinked. How did he know? "Has Shane discussed this with you?" she asked.

Grandfather shook his head. "Sage and I had it all figured out he'd have to marry someone. Problem was, we knew he wouldn't take on just anyone. Then I had this dream just before you came along. The minute we set eyes on you, Sage and I knew you'd been sent."

"Sent?" she faltered.

"Yup. You see, that no-account pa of Sage's got off the booze a couple of years ago, got himself a good job and, I figure, a good woman like my daughter was. I asked a friend who lives down that way to find out who she is, and he says she's got Miwok blood. That's one of the California tribes. I don't say that makes her perfect." He grinned and added, "But I'm prejudiced."

"I still don't see what that has to do with me."

"Look at it from Judge Rankin's side. He might figure Sage should have a chance to be a part of two cultures and here she is living on a Paiute reservation when she could be living with her pa and a new stepmother who's got some of the blood. Two cultures, right there. That's where you come in. The judge looks at you and says, hey, two cultures right here on the res, why move the kid?"

Why you old schemer, she thought, annoyance mixed with amusement. You were planning to marry me off to Shane practically from the moment I walked in the door. And for all I know, even before. No wonder Sage asked if I was married.

"Did you put Shane up to asking me?" she demanded.

He shook his head. "I know better. I might have pointed out how well you and Sage got along, but you can't push that stubborn one."

"Well, he did ask me and I refused."

"Figured you might."

Laura blinked at him. "You didn't think I'd agree?"

"Not till you had some time to think it over. I saw how you got on with Sage—you like her as much as she does you."

"That's true. But, still—marriage is another matter entirely."

"Raised that boy. Never saw him break his word. You set the rules, and he'll stick to 'em."

She stared into Grandfather's wise, dark eyes and decided to confide in him—up to a point. "I couldn't possibly agree to marry *any* man. Not if he expected me to actually *be* his wife."

"You think Shane'd have trouble with that?"

"I don't know," she admitted.

"That's your sticking point, is it? Easy enough to write it out and ask him to sign that he agrees. I'll keep the paper safe. And you'd be safe, too."

Laura bit her lip. Three days ago, she hadn't met any of the Bearclaws. How could she even contemplate such an intimate involvement with Shane, signed agreement or not? And yet, there was Sage to consider. The girl's future mattered a great deal to Laura. She'd never forgive herself if she turned away from this problem and something bad happened to Sage.

Somehow, too, she trusted Grandfather and believed what he'd told her about his grandson. "How long do you think we'd have to keep up the pretense?" she asked.

"According to what you wrote to us about what you're doing with the mustangs, seems to me you're going to be here in the West at least a year."

Laura nodded. "My grant runs for one year, with the possibility of an extension if I find I need a few more months. But I won't be in Nevada all that time. I have to check all the western herds."

"A year sounds pretty good. Sage'll be getting on for twelve by then."

But still vulnerable, Laura thought. After a year, though, the girl's father might well give up any further attempt to gain custody.

"It's not like you're yearning to marry someone else," Grandfather added.

That was true. Even if Laura were gone, there'd be no need to hurry to end the arrangement unless Shane found a woman he could love. And she could always come back and visit Sage from time to time. She wished she could postpone a decision, but realized there wasn't time to shilly-shally. She had to decide now.

"It scares me," she confessed.

"Probably scares the stuffing out of Shane, too," Grandfather countered. "Never saw a man so dead set on not marrying again."

Maybe so, but women were more vulnerable than men in some ways. Could she trust a man she didn't really know? On the other hand, Grandfather trusted him to keep his word, and he'd known Shane from birth.

"It would have to be a very private wedding," she said.

Grandfather smiled at her, then reached for her hand and brought her palm to his chest. "Your words warm my heart," he told her, releasing her hand.

She was touched by his gesture. At the same time she was shaken by the realization that she'd agreed to what seemed to her the wildest scheme in the world. Yet her main emotion was relief that the decision had been made, combined with the surprising sense that she was embarking on an adventure.

Laura shook her head, aware she was the least adventurous person she knew. In some ways, though, she found herself looking forward to this one.

Because of Sage, she assured herself. The girl needed her. Shane certainly didn't, except for legal reasons, and she didn't need him at all. Things really wouldn't be any different between the two of them.

Grandfather rose from his chair. "You bring honor to the Bearclaws," he told her before heading for the back door.

What a strange thing for him to say, though his words had pleased her. She rose and brought the glasses to the sink where she washed them and put them in the drainer. If she was going to live here, it was time to make herself useful. She began assembling the ingredients for the enchiladas, following the recipe Sage had left out for her.

Laura was sliding the chicken enchiladas into the oven when she heard the unmistakable click of Shane's boots. She froze, made a face at herself, and went on with what she was doing, ignoring the panicked hammering of her heart.

When he entered the kitchen she was closing the oven door. Straightening, she blurted, "I told Grandfather we'd get married."

He blinked. Had he changed his mind? Half of her hoped so, but the other, traitorous half waited to hear him say he hadn't.

Shane tried to figure out what to say. Sure, he'd asked her because he couldn't see any other way, but he'd been damn near positive she'd never agree.

"I warned him I expected a private ceremony," she went on.

God knows he did, too. "No problem. Just Grandfather and Sage and the—" He paused. "Never got around to asking. Minister, priest, or justice of the peace?"

"I'd prefer a civil ceremony. A JP will be fine."

He nodded. Seemed more appropriate for the kind of marriage they were heading into.

"Grandfather will keep the paper you sign," she added.

"Paper?"

"Agreeing not to expect me to—well, we'll have separate rooms and such."

Shane watched her flush. He wanted to smile, but was aware he'd better not. "You can be sure I'll never approach you in that way unless—" He paused, watching her as he finished, "—unless you want me to. Unless you decide to move into my bedroom."

"Never!" She made a thrusting away motion with her hands at the same time as the word burst from her.

"I'll sign the paper," he said hastily, sorry to have provoked the distress he saw in her face.

What the hell were they doing, the two of them? Something neither wanted, that was for sure. But he'd do anything to keep Sage and, thankfully, Laura was already fond enough of his sister to agree.

It'd work out, he told himself. It's the right thing to do. But, as he left the kitchen, he had the distinct feeling that old Coyote, the Trickster, was keeping an eye on the pair of them and laughing his head off.

Why shouldn't he be? Getting attached to someone led to trouble. Love led straight to grief, as his first marriage had proved. If he wasn't so fond of his sister, he'd never have gotten himself into this predicament. Here he was, not only having to marry a perfect stranger, but a woman he'd never choose if he really did want a wife.

Later, in bed for the night, he found himself thinking of Laura, sleeping down the hall from him in what would continue to be her bedroom after their marriage. He'd sign her damn paper and abide by what was written, no argument there, but it was beginning to occur to him that part of the deal wasn't going to be as easy as he'd assumed.

It wasn't as though he'd gone without a woman all these years—there were plenty of available women no more interested in marriage than he was. But once he married, it'd be all over the res if he played around. With his custody of Sage in the balance, he couldn't afford to have that happen. No wonder the Trickster laughed—the joke was on Shane Bearclaw.

Laura might not be his type, but she was certainly an attractive woman in her quiet way—any man would agree with that. Yet he'd already given his word he wouldn't touch her, without thinking that he'd be pretty well hobbled when it came to touching any other woman, either. He'd be looking forward to pure frustration.

Unless she changed *her* mind—he'd left that loophole. Chances of that seemed dim. Something about men—he didn't think it was just him— spooked her. It came from her past, and she'd refused to discuss it with him. Which was her privilege. Except now, as he figured it, if she didn't come around to telling him about whatever had happened, she'd remain spooked.

A shame a pretty woman like Laura was so hung up on her past that she couldn't even contemplate making love with any man, even her about-to-be husband, without panicking.

A formidable challenge.

Chapter Four

Laura hadn't realized how easy it was to get married in Nevada—the preliminaries took no time at all. Everything was accomplished during one rainy day. Before she was anywhere near ready to go through with the ceremony, Shane had signed her version of their prenuptial agreement, and they had the marriage license in hand.

Nathan will have a fit, she thought. That was all the more reason not to call ahead of time and tell her brother what she planned to do. It wasn't as though she thought he could talk her out of it. He couldn't. Her mind was made up. But she knew it wasn't going to be easy to try to explain, and so she decided she'd rather put the call off until after the fact.

Determined as she was to go through with this wedding, she couldn't help feeling uncertain. Oddly enough, she realized, the only one in the world who might possibly understand was the man she was about to marry. He must feel equally unsure.

As she and Shane drove into Reno with Grandfather and Sage, Laura hoped she'd be able to calm herself enough to make the proper responses to the justice of the peace.

"My friends think it's way cool that I'm getting a sister-in-law," Sage said from the back of the extended cab on the pickup. "Donna thinks her older sister, Jessica, is going to be jealous, too, 'cause she used to have a crush on Shane."

"This is your idea of keeping it quiet?" Shane asked.

"I only told my two best friends," Sage countered.

"Which means it's all over the res by now."

"They got to know sometime," Grandfather said.

"I suppose," Shane muttered.

Laura wasn't particularly disturbed. Naturally, people on the reservation would find out and it might as well be sooner rather than later. Luckily, her brother, over in Tourmaline, wasn't likely to hear anything until she called and told him—something she wasn't looking forward to.

"I'm so excited!" Sage exclaimed. "I bet you are, too, Laura."

"I'm a little nervous," Laura admitted.

"About being my sister-in-law?"

Laura turned and smiled at her. "That's the best part."

Sage looked pleased but dubious. "Shane wouldn't tell me where you're going on your honeymoon."

What was she supposed to say to that? Laura wondered. Even though Sage, along with Grandfather, felt she'd engineered this marriage, the girl's mind was full of romantic notions about it.

"Laura has to finish her work here," Shane put in. "So we'll be camping out."

"I guess that's better than nothing," Sage told him. "But I thought people always went someplace glamorous."

"Hey, brat, we live next to glamorous Reno, don't we?"

Sage made a face at him. "Reno's just a big town with a bunch of casinos. What's glamorous about that? Lake Tahoe's pretty, though. And close, so it wouldn't take long to get there. It's just up the mountain."

Laura, taking her cue from Shane, said, "I can't afford to take any time away from my work, Sage. Camping it is."

Sighing, Sage said, "If I ever get married, I'm going to New Zealand on my honeymoon. Or maybe Australia."

"After you finish college and get a job," Laura said, "you can go to those places by yourself without having to wait for a honeymoon."

Sage digested that for a moment before asking,

"Know what I'm going to be?" Without waiting for an answer, she added, "A vet, an animal doctor. Grandfather says I got a way with animals."

Listening to Sage chatter distracted Laura enough so she wasn't a complete basket case by the time they reached Reno. Since getting married was the farthest thing from her mind when she had packed to come to Nevada, she'd brought nothing really appropriate to get married in.

She was wearing a cream-colored silk suit, the closest to white she had with her. Not that she wanted a wedding gown for the occasion—heavens, no—but for some reason she'd felt it was important to wear white.

Shane had on what she thought of as a western outfit—black pants and a white shirt with a silver and turquoise bolo tie. And dress boots, in contrast to those he rode with. His long hair was tied back with a black thong adorned with a small beaded ornament she knew Sage had made for him.

In that outfit, he was one of the most striking men Laura had ever seen. Not that his good looks made her any more eager to marry him.

When they piled out near the building that housed the offices of the justice of the peace, Grandfather handed Shane a small box, which he offered to Laura. Inside were four white rosebuds worked into a small bouquet.

Her throat tightened at this unexpected gesture of thoughtfulness, making it hard for her to thank him.

"Four is the mystic number of our people,"

Shane told her. ''I figure we need all the luck we can get.''

He was right, Laura thought, as she gently touched the rosebuds.

''Besides, there are four of us,'' Sage pointed out.

Laura glanced at Sage. The girl knew the reason why she was here, why she was marrying a man she scarcely knew, why she was marrying at all when she'd never intended to. Seeing Sage all but bursting with enthusiasm and joy, though, made it easier for Laura to go on with what must be done.

Once they were in the presence of the justice, Laura caught Grandfather's gaze and he nodded slightly, his dark eyes telling her that, difficult as it might be, she was doing the right thing.

Yes, she was. Or she wouldn't be here. Clasping the rosebud bouquet in front of her, conscious of Shane close beside her, but unable to look at him, she stared straight ahead, willing the ceremony to be over quickly.

When it came time for her to hold out her hand for the ring, the justice had to repeat his words before she understood. Laura had forgotten all about a ring. Shane, though, obviously hadn't because, when she held out her left hand, he slid one onto her ring finger. Glancing down at the wide gold circlet with a center diamond and four small sapphires to either side, she fought back tears.

How could Shane have known sapphires were her birthstone? When she remembered telling Sage her birthday was in September, she still felt all choked up. Obviously he'd asked his sister to find out for him.

She looked up at him, and his lips brushed over hers, a gentle touch that didn't alarm her. To be honest, she rather liked the brief contact.

"That's not how Hank kissed Paula when they got married," Sage informed them as they were leaving. "He kissed her so long we all thought he wasn't ever going to quit."

"I'm not Hank," Shane muttered.

"For which we offer thanks," Grandfather added.

When they were once again in the extended cab truck, Laura tried to decide what to say about the ring. Since it was a wedding ring, as opposed to an engagement ring, she wondered if she should give it back to Shane when they ended the marriage. Or would that be tacky?

Finally she said softly, "The ring is beautiful. And so are the roses. Thank you."

He glanced at her, his eyes enigmatic. For a moment she couldn't look away and, when he finally broke the contact by turning the key and starting the pickup, she found she'd been holding her breath.

"I'm going to be like you," Sage piped up from the back. "I'm going to keep my last name if I ever get married. I'm going to stay a Bearclaw forever and ever. Walker's a pretty good name, though. I can see why you hung onto it."

Yes, she was still Laura Walker, even though she wore a ring that bound her by marriage to Shane Bearclaw. She ran a finger over the stones in the ring and sighed. He was more thoughtful than she'd supposed, this man who was and was not her husband.

"To be a Walker among our people," Grandfather said, "means a person who has a strong spirit within a strong body. A Walker is a special person, one who can see with the spirit what needs to be done and then has the strength to do it. You did well, Laura, to keep your name."

His words circled in her mind. Never before had she really thought about her name having any particular meaning. Though she wasn't one of his people, she felt fortified by what he'd told her.

If everything went as well as the ceremony, perhaps this wouldn't be the ordeal she'd feared it might be. With this in mind, she began to relax. Tomorrow, she thought, I'll get on with my work among the mustangs.

The first clue Laura had that something was amiss was the number of cars parked near the ranch.

"Damn," Shane muttered. "You and your big mouth, sis."

"Whoa," Sage said. "I didn't know so many people were coming."

"So many people?" Shane repeated ominously. "So you knew something was up."

"Well, Donna's mother thought you and Laura needed some kind of a wedding reception," Sage admitted.

"Lot of horses in the corral," Grandfather observed as they pulled into the yard. "Some of 'em rode over."

"It's all right," Laura said, tamping down her rising apprehension at having to play a part in front of Shane's friends. "I'm sure everyone is just being friendly."

"That better be what they have in mind," Shane growled.

What else could it be? Laura wondered.

No sooner had they parked and climbed out of the truck than, amidst wild whoops, men swarmed from the barn. Three of them grabbed Laura. She heard Shane cursing behind her as they bore her off toward the corral. Fear sent bile into her throat. What was happening? She was too scared to struggle.

The next she knew, one of the men mounted a horse and the other two slung her on the horse in back of him. As her captor pounded away from the ranch, she hung onto him for dear life, knowing she'd be thrown off if she didn't.

Dear God, she was being kidnapped!

Again.

Terror numbed her, making her close her eyes and retreat as she had so many years ago, into a small and secret corner of her mind. She was only vaguely aware of the pounding of hooves, shouts and, finally, being jerked from the horse and held against a male body.

"Get the hell out of here!" the man who held her snarled.

"We were only—" the kidnapper said.

"Go!" her new captor growled. "Now!"

She heard the creak of a saddle as someone mounted, the sound of horses trotting away. She kept her eyes closed. To open them was to be smothered in fear. She tried to keep herself stiff, but her legs gave way, and she slumped against the man holding her.

She felt him sit down so that she was on his lap. "Laura," he said softly, "it's all right. You're safe with me."

He called her Laura. That was wrong. The bad man had never called her Laura, he called her Laurie.

His hand stroked her back, slow and gentle. "Open your eyes," he murmured so low she could hardly hear him. "I promised never to hurt you, don't you remember?" On and on his voice crooned soothing words at her, sometimes in a language she didn't understand.

Bit by bit she began to recognize his voice. From the darkness a name flared like a beacon into her mind. Shane. She was with Shane. He was holding her. She wasn't a child, she was a grown woman.

Laura opened her eyes.

In her dilated pupils, Shane saw the dregs of terror, and a muscle twitched in his jaw while he fought to keep his face impassive, his voice as low and gentle as if he were calming a frightened mare. He kept on lightly stroking her back.

"You're safe," he repeated. "You're with me. The other guy is gone. We'll stay here as long as you need to. No one is going to trouble or alarm you. Everything is all right.''

He watched the confusion and fear slowly clear from her face, noting the exact moment recognition seeped into her gaze, which had been fixed on him. ''Sh-Shane?'' she whispered.

He smiled. At no time had his hold on her been binding. Now he loosened his grip even more, so she had the choice of freeing herself easily. He stopped stroking her back.

She blinked and looked around, taking in their surroundings, mostly sagebrush, with his horse standing patiently a few feet away.

''They—those men—'' she faltered.

''They didn't mean to harm you,'' he told her. ''They had no idea they'd scare you.'' Though he kept his voice even, inside he seethed with anger at the damage they'd unknowingly caused.

''But they—they grabbed me,'' she quavered.

''If I'd known ahead of time, I'd have prevented this from happening. What they were doing is an old custom among my people—a fake capture of the bride, with the groom riding to the rescue. I tried to stop them, but I was too late.''

''Oh,'' she said.

He knew her mind was clearing because he could tell she was thinking this information over. He wasn't surprised when, a few moments later, she eased off his lap and got to her feet. He rose quickly, ready to steady her if she faltered, but was careful not to touch her.

"A Paiute custom," she said.

"Not necessarily among all of our people, but here, yes. It was unfortunate word got out about the marriage."

"We can't blame Sage," she said and began brushing dust and debris from her skirt.

Relieved she was recovering, he dusted himself off, then said, "We'll have to ride together on Cloud. I'll put you up first and then sit ahead of you."

She glanced from him to the horse. "At least this time I'll know who I'm holding onto."

The tinge of asperity in her voice pleased him. Whatever past terror the false kidnapping had evoked in Laura, she was rapidly returning to her normal self. He'd figured she'd be scared, but nothing had prepared him for the way he'd found her when he caught up with that joker and rescued her.

It hadn't taken him long to realize Laura had gone beyond panic into some kind of protective trance state. He'd been reminded of young mustang mares who sometimes went into a terror state called capture myopathy during roundups. Those mares often died. Laura had scared him damn near witless.

It might have been scary for her, he didn't deny that, but she'd been far more frightened than he could have predicted. The reason for her panic must be buried in her past. Quite possibly from whatever it was that had fueled her determination never to marry.

He was grateful his instinctive actions, similar to

those he used on panicked mustangs, had brought her back to herself, but he wondered if he'd ever learn the secret to the terror in her past. His new wife was not prone to confiding in her new husband.

"Up you go," he said, boosting her into position on Cloud. He swung up himself, allowing her time to adjust her seating so he could settle into the saddle. "Hang on," he told her as he turned Cloud, heading the gelding toward the ranch.

"I must look a mess," she said, her words muffled by her speaking them more or less into his back as she clung to him. "I can't possibly face all those people."

He decided what she really meant was that she was worried that the men who'd abducted her would realize how panicked she'd been, and she didn't want to face them.

"No one expects the bride to be picture perfect after such a wild ride," he assured her. "Besides, they don't know you, or why we married. They're all dying of curiosity."

He felt, rather than heard, her sigh. "I can't."

"Okay. No problem. I don't blame you for feeling shaky." It certainly wasn't her fault.

Actually, she wasn't nearly so shaken as she had been, Laura realized. Once Shane had gotten through to her and made her understand she wasn't in danger and never had been, the darkness had vanished. Still, she really didn't want to face a bunch of curious strangers.

Strangers who were Shane's friends, she realized

belatedly. Grandfather's friends. Friends of Sage. She'd be letting down the entire Bearclaw family if she scuttled into her room and hid. She might not *be* a Bearclaw, but she'd married one, for whatever reason, and the least she could do was to be courteous enough to meet their friends. No matter how she'd felt about it, those men who'd grabbed her had meant no harm. They were merely following an old custom.

"Give me a few minutes in my room to put myself back together, and I'll join you," she told him. If she was to confront people who must wonder why on earth Shane had married her, she meant to look her best.

At the ranch, Shane surprised her by picking her up and carrying her across the threshold, then all the way to her bedroom, where he left her. Ruffled by this—surely not a Paiute custom—it took her a minute or two to realize her silk skirt, never intended for riding, had split up the back seam. His carrying her had saved her the embarrassment of showing her underwear to the guests.

Quickly she changed into a long, dark-blue skirt and matching lighter-blue shirt, brushed her hair, checked her makeup, took a deep breath, and let it out slowly. She hadn't quite gotten over her reaction to the fake abduction, but she'd learned over the years that inner quaking didn't show.

To her pleased relief, she found Shane waiting for

her in the hall. "Thought we'd present a united front," he said, offering her his arm.

As she placed her hand on his arm, she wondered if he felt as reluctant to face the guests as she did. He'd be forced to play the part of the happy groom in front of his friends while she actually had the easier role because she was a stranger to those people out there. If she were quiet, they wouldn't think it was because the wedding was a sham, but more than likely attribute her behavior to the surprise abduction.

As they joined the crowd in the living room, Sage reached them first to introduce her friend Donna. Donna's mother Rhonda was close behind, and she hugged Laura. Shane nodded and left her with the woman.

"I told those men not to do that," Rhonda said. "I bet you were scared half to death."

"You're right," Laura told her.

"If Shane had told us ahead of time we could have taken you aside and warned you. But he always was one to keep secrets. Imagine him keeping you hidden all this time."

Having no idea what Rhonda meant by "all this time," Laura merely smiled.

"Anyway, we're glad someone finally corralled that cagey old mustang," Rhonda added. "He says you're going to be pretty busy the next few weeks with your work, but when you have the time, we'll get together. There's a powwow coming up, and I know you'll want to help with that—Sage is one of our best dancers."

Whoa, Laura wanted to say, and *not* with the meaning Sage gave the word. Just a little minute here. But she couldn't and still maintain the happy bride illusion. "I'll do whatever Sage wants me to," she temporized.

"Do you sew?" Rhonda asked.

Laura shook her head. "I embroider a bit. I'm afraid I'm rather rusty, though."

"Great." Rhonda turned to two women standing nearby. "Laura embroiders—we've got ourselves a live one."

Wondering what she'd gotten herself into, Laura smiled through the introductions to those women, then to the others, not able to keep everyone straight.

Shane returned, balancing two plates of food, and inclined his head toward the couch, being vacated by another couple. Though not too sure she felt like eating, Laura followed him and discovered she was hungry.

Eventually everyone left. The three men who'd staged the abduction apologized to her before leaving. Laura stood on the front porch with Shane and watched them ride off.

Sage joined them, saying "I guess you're mad at me."

Laura put an arm around her. "Not me."

They both looked up at Shane.

"I'd be a lot more annoyed if I didn't know you meant well," Shane told his sister.

"To make up for it, Grandfather's taking me to a movie right now," Sage said. "That'll give you time to be alone, even if you aren't going on a honey-moon.''

"But—'' Laura began, then paused. She couldn't tell Sage the last thing she wanted was to be alone with her new husband. Grandfather must know better, though.

"So—see you later,'' Sage said, and scooted away.

Shane and Laura looked at each other. She decided the rueful expression on his face must match her own and, for some reason, that struck her funny. How often did both bride and groom dread being alone together? A giggle escaped her.

He began to chuckle and, moments later, both of them were laughing fit to kill.

When they quieted down, Shane said, "One of my friends brought champagne. The least we can do is drink a toast to what must be the most reluctant bride and groom in the state of Nevada.''

"Possibly in the entire country,'' she said.

He waved toward the chairs on the porch. "I'll bring it out here. Going to be an awesome sunset.''

Later, sipping her champagne, Laura watched the evening clouds gradually turn salmon pink as the sun lowered toward the mountains to the west. She actually felt relaxed and comfortable, which she'd never expected, given the strain of the wedding, and then the trauma of the abduction. Shane was an easy man to be with, one reason being he didn't talk unless he had something that needed to be said.

"I don't know when I last watched a sunset," she murmured.

"Heals the spirit," he told her.

She decided he was right.

Unexpectedly, he reached for her left hand. Because his movement was slow and easy, she didn't jerk away. He held her hand lightly, his fingers touching the ring.

"The four stones on the left are you and me, plus Sage and Grandfather," he said. "The ones on the right are the four mystic numbers of my people."

"And the diamond?"

"That represents our union."

A thrill shot through her. Denying it, she took her hand from his and said, "But it's not a true union."

"For whatever reason, we are joined, you and I." His voice was low and soft. "I'll honor my written agreement, but though our bodies and our spirits remain separate, we are bound together."

His words eased inside her, lodging in her heart. She shivered—not from fear, more from the feeling that what she'd heard was a prophecy.

United. Bound together.

What had she done?

Chapter Five

The next morning, Laura and Shane packed their gear and rode out early. Despite her misgivings, Laura had slept soundly and, if she'd dreamed, she didn't remember doing so.

They loped along in silence until she finally said, "I'm going to have to call my brother and let him know we're married."

"Your brother?" Shane echoed.

Only then did she realize she'd never even mentioned having a brother, much less one who lived in Nevada, not all that far away from the reservation.

"Nathan's a doctor in Tourmaline," she said. "I didn't want to tell him ahead of time because, well—" she faltered.

Shane didn't prompt her, he just waited.

"He'd have tried to talk me out of it, and I didn't want to cope with that hassle along with everything else," she admitted finally.

He slanted a look her way. "Could he have changed your mind?"

She shook her head. "Once my mind's made up, I stick to my decisions. Getting this government grant was one of them. I was in a boring job that under-utilized my abilities, and I realized I had to do something else."

"A safe job." It wasn't a question.

He was right. Safe but boring. Like her life—up until now.

"Is your brother married?" Shane asked.

"To Jade Adams."

"She's Adams Drilling, right?"

"Oh, do you know Jade?"

"Never met her. Heard about her. Pretty much everyone in the area knows who runs Adams Drilling. Her crew's dug wells on the res."

"I think maybe Jade might understand," Laura said. "But not Nathan. He knows I planned never to marry and now to have rushed into it so suddenly…"

"Swept you off your feet."

Seeing his wry grin, she said, "Literally, if not figuratively, courtesy of that mustang stallion."

"You'll be telling him the truth?"

"He's my brother."

"That's not an answer. What will you tell him?"

Laura chewed her lip. "I have to think about how I'm going to word it."

"How about your parents? You've never mentioned them."

"They travel a lot. I guess that comes from my father being an engineer before he retired. I want to talk to Nathan before I decide what to tell them. There's no hurry since they're in the Far East at the moment. My dad's fascinated with that big dam the Chinese are building."

Laura knew she was chattering, but couldn't help herself. What *was* she going to tell her folks?

"I don't usually act on impulse," she added. "Applying for the government grant was the first time I can remember doing anything on the spur of the moment."

"And I'm the second?"

"I'd put it a bit differently—helping you out in order to protect Sage might be called a spur-of-the-moment decision."

"No might involved—it damn well was. I was surprised you followed through."

"So was I." Involuntarily she glanced down at her ring. "How did you know my ring size?" she asked abruptly.

"Carving's given me a good eye for what will fit what. When do you plan to tell your brother?"

She could hardly say she'd like to put it off as long as possible. "Soon."

"Any other relatives I should know about?"

"Nathan and Jade have an adopted son named

Tim. They're sort of accidental parents, but Tim's a darling. And then Jade has two brothers. One's a rancher in Carson Valley.''

She sighed, wondering what Zed Adams and his wife were going to make of her hasty wedding. There seemed to be no end to the explanations she was going to have to come up with.

Feeling much like Scarlet O'Hara in *Gone With The Wind* she decided she'd think about what to say to all her Nevada relatives tomorrow—or even later.

She deliberately changed the subject, asking, ''Where do you think we might find mustangs today?''

''We'll try one of the stud piles.''

''The what?''

''Stallions do that. Got the whole desert to use, but any one of them with a harem makes a pile of manure, coming back to the same place time after time. Marking territory. If we don't find any horses near the pile, then we'll think about picking a good campsite by a stream. Let 'em come to us.''

Camp. She'd agreed to camping, and she wasn't about to back down, but the idea of being really isolated with Shane at night rattled her cage. He'd promised to abide by the agreement he'd signed but he was, after all, a man. One she was married to, furthermore.

She cleared her throat. ''About the tent,'' she began.

''Like I said—it's for you. I prefer sleeping under the stars.''

"I know, but what if it rains?"

He shot her an exasperated look. "The day I can't foresee a storm coming, that's the day I deserve to get wet. Besides, it rarely rains here in June. I am *not,* repeat, *not* about to creep into your tent like some old-time movie sheik."

A picture of Zed's brother Talal popped into her head and, before she could stop herself, Laura giggled. "He is one," she said. "A sheik, I mean. Jade's brother Talal."

Shane raised his eyebrows. There seemed to be no end to the relatives Laura kept bringing up. "Try drawing me a family tree," he suggested.

She threw herself into an explanation that seemed to be a confused tangle until he realized it was her sister-in-law's relatives who had tangled pasts. Brothers raised in two separate countries?

"Okay, I've got it straight," he said at last. "They didn't know until recently that each other existed because they were separated so young. One was left behind in Kholi, and one was raised in the U.S."

He did, more or less. Now he knew there were at least two men he'd have to face sooner or later—her brother and Zed Adams. Maybe Talal Zohir as well, if he hadn't returned to his mideastern country, and possibly some government agent who seemed to be related to Zed's wife but didn't actually live in Nevada.

His plan had seemed so simple at first, involving only Laura and him. But as Grandfather had more than once pointed out, no act was without unforeseen consequences. After a pebble was dropped into a pool, the waves kept spreading.

"You'd do well to talk to your brother as soon as possible," he said. "The information highway around here may be word of mouth, but it's more efficient than you'd believe."

She sighed. "I probably should have told Nathan before. It still doesn't seem real to me—the marriage, I mean."

But it was real. Otherwise why would he be feeling responsible for Laura? He'd been furious with those so-called friends of his yesterday when they'd staged the abduction of the bride. And even more so after he'd rescued her and seen the state she was in.

Like Sage, he'd always had a way with animals and tried to help when he found one frightened or hurt. But Laura was no animal, she was his wife, and it troubled him to realize her terror had been out of proportion to the frightening incident. He felt a driving need to erase whatever had caused that overwhelming panic.

First, though, she'd need to trust him enough to share her past with him. Considering her wariness with men—not just with him, he'd noticed—any sharing wasn't likely to be soon.

They visited the stud pile without seeing a single mustang. Later, as the sun began to edge downward, he found the exact camp spot he'd been looking for.

Without being asked, Laura helped him set up the tent, but when it seemed she intended to help him with the evening meal, he drew the line.

"Inside, cook all you want," he said. "Outside, it's my job."

She eyed him for a moment. "I suppose you'll let me clean the dishes afterward, though."

He shook his head. "Outside, I'll do it. Inside, that's up to you and Sage."

"Division of labor, Shane's way? Any other dos and don'ts I should be aware of?" Her tone was challenging.

He shrugged. "Most are open to arbitration. Grandfather and I haven't had a woman in the house for a long time. Sage does her best, but she's still a kid. They got laws about overworking ten-year-olds. You, now, are a full-grown woman so you're fair game."

With hidden amusement he watched her start to puff up indignantly, then stop and shake her head ruefully, saying, "I almost walked into that one. I can see getting to know you is going to be tricky."

"I'm an open book."

"Going by that last statement of yours, I'd have to say it must be a joke book."

He wanted to tell her life wasn't all that grimly serious, that she needed to kick back and relax, but he knew she wasn't ready to listen.

Once they'd eaten, they sat on a blanket near the dying fire. The silence between them felt comfortable to him, but he wondered if she was still uneasy about the night to come. He'd never forced himself on any woman, and he sure as hell wasn't about to start with her.

"There's something about a campfire that's mesmerizing," she said finally. "Inside a house, an open fire isn't quite the same."

"Nothing's the same inside." Not even making love, he was tempted to add, but didn't. Somehow, he doubted Laura had ever made love in the outdoors. When it occurred to him he'd like to be the one to show her the possibilities, he clamped down on the thought, eradicating it.

"The moon's coming up. I can see it between the cottonwood branches," she said.

A quarter moon, waxing.

The chuckling howl of a coyote drifted on the cool evening breeze, reminding Shane that the Trickster might not be through with him yet. Wait until the moon was full and he had to lie under it alone, with Laura not far away but as difficult to reach as a princess in a tower.

"Listen," she said, "another coyote is answering the first one. I always look forward to hearing them."

He'd been wrong about her tenderfoot status. The way she helped him set up the tent told him she'd done it before. She rode a fair distance without tiring, knew how to take care of a horse, and was not spooked by the coyotes' chorus. He'd yet to hear her complain about anything except the mustangs' elusiveness.

Look at the way she'd pulled herself together and faced the crowd at the impromptu reception yesterday. No one besides him could have guessed how much willpower that must have taken. He was beginning to appreciate the capabilities of his new wife. She might look fragile, but she possessed an inner strength he couldn't help but admire.

Stealing a glance at Shane's impassive profile, Laura wished she wasn't so afraid of him touching her. Actually, the few times he'd done so had been rather pleasant. Although, come to think about it, pleasant was a non-specific word like nice. Not really the right word to describe the feelings she'd had.

But she'd best not dwell on those feelings with the night still ahead of her. A vision of Shane attired in one of Talal's Arab robes while he crept sheik-like toward her tent made her smile. In her heart she knew he wouldn't, in or out of Arab robes. And yet she was nervous.

Never in her life had she been in such a position—alone in an isolated camp with a man she wasn't related to. Of course, if marriage counted, in a way she *was* related to Shane. It might help if she could think of him as a brother.

That made her roll her eyes. No way.

A friend? She'd never had a male friend and wasn't sure she could ever manage such a friendship.

''I wonder what your friends thought about the marriage,'' she said.

"Our marriage? The guys figured my luck was running high. Rhonda told me it was about time."

She'd noticed he'd changed her "the" to "our" but decided to ignore it. "No broken hearts among the women?"

He grinned at her. "Who knows?"

She made a face at him.

Mournful hoots from somewhere among the trees startled her into turning to look.

"Moohoo'oo," Shane said. "The night flyer is heard but not seen."

"Owl," she said. "Your word fits him perfectly. Which reminds me—Sage said you were learning to be a medicine man."

"It's not something to be acquired overnight, but Grandfather thinks I might make the grade, in time."

She wanted to ask him more, but wasn't sure her questions would be welcome. Maybe when she knew him better. "I think I'll turn in," she said, trying for a casual tone. "See you in the morning."

Watching Laura head for the tent, Shane shook his head. He hadn't missed the little quaver in her voice. He hoped she'd soon realize she was safe with him. It was not only disconcerting to have an attractive woman afraid of him, but he hated to see her on edge.

After packing up in the morning, they rode back toward the ranch. The camp-out had been, for him, sort of a trial run to see how Laura reacted. Now that he knew she was okay with trail camps, they could stay out several days at a time.

On the way in, they caught sight of the small bachelor herd but no other mustangs. He figured the others must be off to the north and that well might be a two- to three-day camp, so that's what he'd plan for next.

They came in sight of the house near noon, and he frowned when he saw an unfamiliar car parked in the drive. He was about to comment on it when he heard Laura draw in her breath.

"Oh, good heavens," she muttered. "That looks like my brother's car."

"The grapevine," he said resignedly.

Sage came running out when they halted at the corral and dismounted. Unfolding the Reno *Gazette Journal* she held, she thrust it at Shane. "Look, you and Laura made the paper. It says right here that 'according to a colorful Paiute custom, the bride was abducted on horseback and then rescued by the groom.'"

"Names and all?" Laura asked apprehensively.

Sage nodded. "That's why your brother and his wife are waiting for you in the house. They gave me the Reno paper. I think he's kind of mad."

Shane decided that was probably an understatement. "How did the paper get hold of it?"

"Grandfather called around and found out Hank Roan is the new res correspondent. He wasn't at the reception, but his wife was."

Trust Hank to screw things up, Shane thought. "Ask Grandfather to come help you with the horses and gear," he told Sage.

Shane meant to face the music with Laura. She needed his support, whether she realized it or not.

"I should have called Nathan earlier," Laura said distractedly, as they headed for the house. "What a way for him to find out."

Shane could well imagine how he'd go up like a rocket if Sage were older and pulled a stunt like this. Facing Nathan Walker wasn't going to be easy. And he'd heard Jade Adams had a temper to go with her red hair.

Bracing himself, he walked with Laura into the living room. Nathan, standing by the window, hurried to his sister and, taking her hands in his, asked, "Are you all right, sis?"

Laura's smile looked shaky as she released herself. "I'm fine, Nathan, and in full possession of my senses, in case that was your next question." She turned to Shane and surprised him by linking her arm in his. It was the first time she'd voluntarily touched him.

"This is my new husband, Shane Bearclaw. Shane, this is my brother Nathan and his wife, Jade."

The introduction forced a bit of formality into what promised to be an explosive situation as they briefly nodded at one another. Shane saw Nathan take a deep breath but, before he could speak, Jade did.

"Laura, why didn't you let us know?" she asked plaintively.

"It's my fault," Shane said. "I'd hoped we could have a private ceremony, but my little sister told her friends and we returned from Reno to an impromptu reception we didn't realize had been planned. It got out of hand."

"I was going to call you," Laura told her brother.

"When?" he demanded.

"Tonight. I—we—had no idea the Reno paper had picked up on the bride abduction."

"That doesn't explain why you didn't let us know before the fact," Nathan said.

"I'm sure if Shane had known I had a brother, he would have insisted," Laura said. "I didn't tell him about you until today."

She was trying to protect him, Shane realized with amazement. Trying to deflect her brother's anger away from him.

Nathan stared at her. "I don't understand any of this, Laura. It's not like you."

Jade rose from her chair and crossed to stand beside her husband. "Let's all sit down and give Laura time to explain," she suggested.

Shane unobtrusively urged Laura toward the couch so they'd be facing this side by side. Jade seated herself again and they all looked expectantly at Nathan. He scowled, but finally took a chair near his wife.

"Well," Laura began, "this has mostly to do with Sage, Shane's young sister—I think you've met her."

"Sister?" Nathan muttered.

Laura nodded. "She's been living with her brother and Grandfather ever since her mother died two years ago. Recently her father, who's never paid any attention to her since Sage and her mother came to live on the ranch when she was four, remarried and is now seeking custody of his daughter. Sage is happy here and doesn't want to leave the only home she's ever really known." Laura paused and fixed her attention on her brother. "She's also aware her father abused her mother."

"Surely no judge would grant custody to an abusive father," Jade put in indignantly.

"The father is a recovering alcoholic who's been dry for three years now," Laura explained. "The judge handling the case felt Sage might be better off in a two-parent home, even though he knows, likes, and respects Shane."

Did I tell her all that? Shane asked himself. As I recall, I barely mentioned the judge. Must have been Grandfather. He knows everything.

"I just couldn't allow Sage to be exposed to possible abuse," Laura continued. "I'm sure you can understand that. And Shane, well, he and I get along so well we decided to marry to protect his sister."

Shane didn't so much as blink, even though he was startled by the way Laura was presenting their marriage of accommodation. Get along well?

"You married a man you hardly know so he can keep his sister?" Nathan's voice was heavy with disbelief.

"Of course that wasn't all!" Laura sounded positively indignant. "I *like* Shane. We're quite compatible."

"Good for you, Laura," Jade said unexpectedly, causing her husband to stare at her.

"It may not be the usual reason to marry," Jade went on calmly, "but it's one I can understand. I do wish you'd shared this with us ahead of time, though."

"Nathan would've tried to talk me out of it,"

Laura told her. "He couldn't have, but I thought it was simpler to wait until the ceremony was over."

Nathan looked from one woman to the other. "You're condoning this?" he asked his wife.

"When I think of how desperately you and I wanted to keep Tim," she told him, "I can understand Shane's feelings. And Laura's. She's obviously already very fond of the girl, and Shane, too, or she'd never have agreed. Remember, she wasn't coerced into the marriage. It was of her own free will."

Taking a deep breath, Nathan faced Shane squarely. "I don't like it, but I'll accept the marriage, given the reason. Laura is—she's special. I wouldn't want her hurt."

Shane met his measuring gaze. "Your sister is also special to me, Dr. Walker. I give you my word she'll never come to harm at my hands."

He meant every word and, apparently, Nathan realized he did, because he gave a slight nod.

Sage bounded into the room, saying, "I fixed iced tea for everyone. Who likes sugar or sweetener?"

Jade smiled at her. "How nice of you. Plain for me, please."

After that, Nathan could hardly refuse, Shane thought. And he didn't. "Sweetener," he told Sage gruffly.

Laura could have kissed Sage. There was something about accepting food or drink in someone's house that made for cordial exchanges at the very least.

Jade commented on Shane's mustang carving. "I recognized your name when I saw the article in the

Reno paper. My brother Talal has one you did of a hawk. He says it reminds him of the falcons in Kholi. You're very talented.'' Jade's words pleased Laura. Shane was an artist with wood, and she was glad to see others recognized it.

"Laura mentioned your brother today,'' Shane said. "I'm happy Talal enjoys the hawk.''

With a glance at Nathan, Jade said, "We'll have to have you out to Zed's ranch to meet everyone.''

Nathan grunted.

"First though, we're going to ask you to visit us in Tourmaline.'' Jade fixed her gaze on Laura. "Give me a ring to set a time that fits into your schedule.''

"I'll do that,'' Laura said, understanding that whether or not Nathan wanted any further contact with Shane, Jade meant to make sure he was included in the family.

Jade's kindness touched her, but also alarmed her. Their marriage wasn't forever, making it awkward to be accepted into the family as a couple when they really were not. And why had she embroidered the plain facts of their marriage with what were half-truths at the most?

When Nathan and Jade got up to leave, Shane told her brother he was glad they'd met, calling him Dr. Walker.

"Nathan,'' her brother muttered. "I don't answer to "doctor'' except in the office.''

Laura concealed a smile. First names. A small concession, but one all the same.

She reached up and kissed her brother on the cheek, whispering, "It's okay, really. Don't worry.''

He gave her a doubtful smile before following Jade down the porch steps. Laura was about to close the door when she heard Jade say to him, "Don't you see? This guy may be your sister's only chance to be happy."

She stood for a moment with her back to the closed door. Shane, still in the entryway but too far away to have heard Jade's words, asked, "Everything all right?"

"I think so," she said absently, turning over in her mind what her sister-in-law had said.

All that embroidery she'd done around the truth must have been the reason for Jade's words. She'd made it sound to her brother and sister-in-law as though she might have married Shane sometime in the future, anyway. Which of course was a lie.

And she still didn't know why she'd done it.

Her last chance to be happy? Jade's words disturbed her. Happy with a man she had no intention of staying married to?

Chapter Six

As it turned out, the camping expedition had to be postponed because the next morning Shane, as one of the spokesmen for the Pyramid Lake Paiutes, was summoned to a joint meeting with the Walker River Reservation. He told Laura it concerned water rights.

"We may not get through this for a couple of days," he added.

Sage, who'd been listening, said, "That's okay. Now Laura can help me with my powwow stuff."

Laura did want to help Sage, plus she knew there'd be little point in her venturing out alone to look for the mustangs. In any case, though she'd die before admitting it, all that riding had left her a bit stiff. A few days out of the saddle would be welcome.

"I don't mind," she told Shane, meaning it.

He nodded and had started toward the door when Sage asked, "Aren't you even going to kiss Laura goodbye?"

He paused, raising one eyebrow at Laura. Quickly, she offered her cheek but, with a forefinger under her chin, he turned her face and brushed his lips over hers, much as he'd done at the wedding.

Once again, the brief contact triggered a tingling response inside her.

"And don't tell me Hank doesn't do it that way," Shane warned his sister. "That renegade's caused enough problems already."

Watching Shane leave, Laura wondered how she might react if sometime he decided to really kiss her.

Sage, giggling at her brother's parting remark, said, "Hank kisses his wife like he means it. Even if there are other people around. Shane wouldn't ever do that. In front of people, I mean." She paused. "At least I don't think so."

"I wouldn't know," Laura said, then hastily switched topics, asking about the powwow.

"Grandfather says this one is to celebrate the coming of summer. He told me in the olden days the people always danced when the seasons changed. Then it sort of stopped for a while, but now he says we're reclaiming our culture. Some of the boys are learning to make reed duck decoys, and Donna's grandmother's teaching us girls to weave baskets. Whoa, talk about hard! But she says I've got nimble fingers. Only she uses the people's word.''

''So you're learning to speak Paiute, too?''

''I can already do that pretty good 'cause Grandfather taught me when I was little. I'm really, really glad you and Shane got married so I won't ever have to leave here.'' She smiled shyly at Laura. ''I know you're actually my sister-in-law, but it sort of feels like you're my new mother.''

Moved, blinking back threatening tears, Laura said huskily, ''I'm afraid I'm not very good at being a mother.''

''Sure you are. You listen to me lots better than Donna's mother listens to her. And you hug me a lot. Maybe you'll dance with me at the powwow, too.''

Laura blinked. ''Dance with you?''

''I guess you don't know the women always dance separate from the men. One of our dances is for mothers and daughters.''

Although she certainly hadn't planned to be a participant in the powwow, Laura saw now she couldn't refuse. ''But I don't know any of your dances,'' she protested.

''I can teach you. We got two days yet. It's not hard, mostly keeping in step with the drums and rattles. Grandfather's got a drum, and he can play for us while I show you what to do. It's supposed to be a secret, but Donna's mother's already making your costume.''

''She shouldn't have to do that.''

"Well, I think she sort of expects you to embroider her vest."

Laura smiled. A fair trade-off. Whether she'd wished it or not, Shane's community apparently wanted to accept her, and this gave her a warm feeling.

That evening, she found herself missing Shane. She'd known he was staying overnight at the Walker River Reservation, but she hadn't expected to so much as notice his absence. Fond as she was of Sage, and much as she respected Grandfather, it seemed to her as if the heart had gone from the ranch house without Shane there. Which was foolish as well as fanciful.

She was busy enough. Rhonda had come over with Donna in the afternoon to have Laura try on the dress she was making for her, and she'd brought not one, but two vests, along with floral patterns for Laura to embroider on them.

Grandfather, sitting in his usual evening silence in the living room while she worked on the vests, suddenly said, "Do you know what you and Sage are promising when you dance together?"

"I told her it was mother and daughter," Sage commented.

Grandfather gave her a look. Sage rolled her eyes, but kept her mouth shut after that.

"You make a promise to the earth to renew," he said, "as you are renewed in your daughter, as the change of seasons renews all that grows. Sage will

promise to do the same when her time for the renewal vow comes.''

Laura thought it over, not exactly sure what she
could renew but rather liking the idea of a promise
to the earth.

''I'll do my best,'' she told him.

He grinned at her. ''You stay long enough and
we'll make a Paiute out of you, yet.''

''But she *is* going to stay a long time,'' Sage insisted. ''This is her home, too.''

Up until that moment, Laura had assumed Shane
or Grandfather, or maybe both had explained to
Sage about the nature of the marriage—had told her
that once Shane's custody of his sister was secure,
Laura would be leaving. Either no one had done this
or Sage preferred not to believe it.

Sage looked at her, hazel eyes expectant. ''You
are, aren't you?''

Unable to bring herself to tell the girl the blunt
truth, Laura temporized. ''You know I have a job to
do, that all the wild horses aren't here in Nevada.''

''I guess so.'' Sage didn't sound too happy about
it. She remained unusually quiet until Laura claimed
she needed more dancing practice.

Once Grandfather brought out his small drum and
Sage began demonstrating the steps, the girl's usual
exuberance returned. But she hugged Laura extra
hard when they said good-night.

The following night Shane returned. Everybody
had gone to bed except Laura, who'd told herself
she was staying up to finish the embroidery on the

second vest. But the moment she heard Shane's pickup in the driveway, the leap of her heart told her she'd lied. She'd been waiting for him.

In fact, as she hastily put away the embroidery gear, she realized the cookies she'd had Sage and Donna help her bake in the afternoon really had been for his homecoming. She was waiting in the kitchen when he came in the back door.

"Hungry?" she asked.

He offered her his slow, teasing smile. "Depends on what's available."

Heat rose to her face as she tried to ignore what she knew must be his double meaning. Yet what he'd said didn't frighten her. Somehow she'd gotten over any fear of Shane.

"I made some cookies," she said. "And coffee will only take a minute."

Once the coffee was ready she joined him at the table, sipping from her mug as he ate a chocolate-chip cookie. When he started on the second one, she smiled. "I sneaked oatmeal into them."

"Doesn't seem to have ruined them," he said, reaching for another.

"Oatmeal's good for you. It sort of makes up for the not-so-good-for-you chocolate and butter."

He chuckled. "I like your way of thinking."

She searched for the right word to define how it felt sitting here with him, just the two of them, and came up with cozy. Never had she thought to use that word in connection with a man. She didn't even feel cozy with her own brother, for heaven's sake.

"Did your meeting solve anything?" she asked.

He shrugged. "We always hope so. Water rights are a touchy subject in Nevada. Like the mustangs."

"Speaking of mustangs, I don't feel a bit guilty about taking tomorrow off," she said. "I wouldn't miss the powwow for the world. The horses will still be there—wherever they are—the day after. Did you know Sage taught me one of the women's dances? We're going to dance together to welcome summer. I have a costume and everything."

Shane thought she sounded as young and eager as Sage. "I knew you were helping out, but I didn't realize you were going to dance," he said.

"Sage explained about how the women dance separate from the men, and it sounded like fun. Grandfather warned me it's spiritual, and I'm all right with that, too. Earth should be honored by all of us—it's our home."

"You don't have to convince me. I'm dancing, too."

He'd be with the men, of course. What she evidently didn't know was that after the ceremonial dancing was over, there'd be a celebration. With luck, the res combo would be in good form, and there'd be party dancing, meaning couples.

Would she dance with him? Let him hold her close? The idea was arousing. Somehow this don't-touch-me gal had gotten under his skin.

She'd waited up for him tonight. Laura didn't strike him as being particularly dutiful, so he took it as a sign she was beginning to accept him as something other than a male to be feared.

"When we met," he said, "I figured I was being saddled with another typical eastern greenhorn. We get quite a few, off and on, doing some kind of study. Turns out you're not what I thought." He offered her a half-smile. "Turns out I like you."

"After that meeting, I didn't think I'd ever come to like you," she admitted. "But I was wrong."

From her, that was something. "Then I guess you didn't lie to your brother, after all," he said.

"It's getting late," she said, rising and picking up the dishes to take to the counter.

He figured she was retreating from her own realization that she'd begun to like him. Maybe even trust him. He'd been wondering about a good-night kiss, but decided not to risk it. Best to consolidate his gains at this point. She couldn't be rushed any more than you could tame a mustang real quick. It took time, patience, and gentleness.

Which he was willing to allow. The problem was his body didn't seem to be working in sync with his mind.

"I'm tired myself," he said, which was more or less true. Getting up from the table he touched her lightly on the shoulder. "See you in the morning."

Her "good night" sounded relieved.

Morning was a rush of preparation for the pow-wow. Much of what the men wore to dance went on over their ordinary clothes, so Shane was dressed pretty much as usual in jeans and a T-shirt, except for the moccasins on his feet. Grandfather had on his beaded buckskin outfit, worn only for ceremonials, and wore his hair in two braids.

Laura had braided ribbons into Sage's long hair and had her own shorter hair done up in what Shane recognized as a French braid. The sight of her in the dance costume of his people touched a chord in him that he hadn't realized existed. It had nothing to do with lust, attractive as she looked. This went deeper, and he wasn't sure he could find a name for it.

"Sage says we need to bring other clothes for afterwards," Laura told him, "so I'm taking this flight bag."

He nodded. "Good idea. Let's hit the road."

The community center was already bursting with sounds and color. There was nothing drab about powwows. The good smell of Indian bread cooking made Shane's mouth water. Outside, booths offering other food and handmade items flanked the dance arena. Obsidian wind chimes tinkled in the warm breeze, mingling with the sound of gourd rattles shaken by toddlers.

Someone blew an eagle whistle, so high-pitched as to hurt the ears. Another was drumming, changing rhythms with smooth speed.

"I had no idea it would be like this," Laura said. "I can't make up my mind what to look at first."

"Come and meet Donna's sister Jessica," Sage said to Laura. "She flew in for the powwow, and she's going to dance, too."

Shane had already been hailed by some of the men and was talking to them, so Laura followed Sage, recalling that the girl had told her before that this sister used to have a crush on Shane. It made her wonder how Jessica would react to his new wife.

They found Jessica braiding ribbons into Donna's hair in the Patsona family camper. Laura, who'd pictured her as nineteen or twenty, was surprised to see she was older, maybe about her own age. Even more surprising, Jessica was stunning—tall and dark, with eyes as green as cottonwood leaves.

"They tell me you breached the Bearclaw defenses," Jessica said to her after they were introduced. "I hear he succumbed without so much as a whimper."

Laura found herself momentarily speechless. If Shane needed a wife, why on earth wouldn't he have wanted to marry this gorgeous creature?

Jessica laughed. "I don't mean to embarrass you. But your coup did set the entire res agog, you know."

Finding nothing appropriate to say about her marriage to Shane, Laura changed the subject. "Sage said you flew in for the powwow. Where are you living now?"

"Albuquerque at the moment. My San Francisco-based company sends me wherever they need an MBA to straighten things out. It doesn't pay for me to buy or rent a place—I just come home here between assignments."

An MBA? "If you'd asked me what I thought you did, I'd have said modeling," Laura said honestly.

"Modeling did help me get through college." Jessica made a face. "It's such an unreal life, though. Numbers, now, they're something to hold onto." She finished the braiding and Donna flashed her sister a smile before hurrying off with Sage.

"I'm really glad Shane found you," Jessica said. "I gave up on him long ago when I saw how he'd closed himself off." She glanced through the open back door of the camper, lowered her voice and then added, "It was all due to that cheating wife of his— a regular little res blanket-warmer she turned out to be. It wasn't surprising he decided women weren't to be trusted."

Laura swallowed. All she'd known about his wife was that she was dead. No wonder he hadn't wanted to marry again.

"I see you didn't know what she was like," Jessica said.

"No."

"Anyway, it's good he's come out of his shell and great for Sage to have the big sister she's always wanted. She's a neat kid. You'll be good for both of them."

Jessica spoke with such candor that Laura decided she really wasn't carrying a torch for Shane.

"Are *you* considering getting married?" she asked.

Jessica shook her head. "I'm not ready to settle

down. Anyway, I haven't met the wild and wonderful man of my dreams yet.''

Laura smiled at her, liking this blunt and beautiful woman. "I hope you meet him unexpectedly in some wild and wonderful place.''

"That won't be Albuquerque, I'm afraid.'' Jessica glanced at her watch. "I'd better get into my dancing clothes.''

"I'm going to look around before the dancing begins,'' Laura said. "This is my first powwow, and I don't want to miss anything.''

"See you later, then,'' Jessica told her. "I'm glad we met.''

"So am I.'' Laura spoke the truth.

As she left the camper, she smiled to herself, thinking about the last part of their conversation. She and Shane had certainly met unexpectedly. To her, Northern Nevada was both wild and wonderful. And Shane? Since she didn't want *any* man, she'd never conjured up a dream man. But if she had, he might have been a bit like Shane.

Later, dancing with Sage and the other women, Laura concentrated at first on not making a misstep, but soon, in harmony with the beating drums, she began to relax, freeing her mind to think about the meaning of what she was doing. *Renewal,* Grandfather had said. There hadn't been much of that in her life, but maybe finding the courage to apply for and get that government grant had been a form of renewal.

What unexpected results had come from it!

She couldn't understand the chants, but assumed they had to do with the earth, and so she made up one for herself, blending it in with the rest, getting so carried away she wasn't even sure what she'd said. Or was it promised? Promise was the word Grandfather had used.

The marriage ceremony had pretty much been a blur to her, but, as she recalled, there was something in it about promising to love and honor. The thought troubled her.

Honor was easy enough. Shane was certainly worthy of honor. But love? How could it ever be possible for her to love any man?

Though she enjoyed being a part of the dancing, it had stirred up troublesome thoughts that made her glad when the women finished and men began.

She'd intended to go and examine some of the crafts, but she found herself, with most of the other women, watching the men. She, though, focused solely on Shane. The male dancers used a different step, the drums throbbed with a quicker tempo, and the dance itself had a certain wild aspect the women's dance had lacked.

Shane, who'd led the dancers into the arena, was magnificent in a beaded headdress that held a single eagle feather. Unlike the Native Americans from the Plains, the Paiutes didn't wear warbonnets. Like the other men, his face was painted with alternating lines of black and red, no two faces painted quite the same.

He looked totally unlike the man she'd married. A wild and wonderful stranger danced before her, speeding her heartbeat, making her breath come short and totally bemusing her.

She had no idea how long she'd stood watching him before Sage startled her by taking her hand.

"I'm getting hungry," the girl said. "Shane always lets me buy tacos—they're really good here. Donna told me we got some buffalo meat from friends in Montana so the tacos'll be awesome this time."

Shaking off the spell of Shane's dance, Laura allowed Sage to lead her to the booth area. Sitting at a picnic table under an awning eating tacos and drinking orange soda, Laura shook off the shards of the spell.

"These are fabulous," she told Sage. "I've never tasted buffalo meat before."

When the men finished dancing, the children danced—boys and girls separately. After that, there was a break before the women danced again, and then the men.

Laura and Sage changed from their dance costumes in the dressing room in the community building. Because Laura had brought a skirt, Sage had insisted on one, too. It was flattering that the girl wanted to imitate her, but scary, too. What kind of a role model was she for a ten-year-old child?

Since her hair was straggling down from the

French braid, Laura undid the braid and brushed her hair until it settled loosely onto her shoulders.

Sage bit her lip as she watched obviously undecided about her own hair.

"I think the ribbons in your braids look really cool," Laura told her.

Examining herself in the mirror, Sage finally nodded. "I guess I'll leave the braids in, then."

"That's good, 'cause I'm gonna leave mine in," Donna said, coming up to make a face at Sage in the mirror. "You know that cool guy from Walker River? The one that's Joe Roan's cousin? I heard him say he thought you were cute."

Sage's hazel eyes sparkled. "Honest?"

Donna nodded. "Wanna go look for them?"

Laura sighed inwardly. Only ten and thrilled because a boy thought she was cute. Sage needed a mother around to make sure she learned there were other things more important in life than being cute.

"Don't go wandering too far off," she told the girls.

They nodded, and hurried away, giggling. Laura gave herself one last look before leaving the room. She'd never be as striking as Jessica, but she wasn't bad. And Shane had chosen her when he might have, at one time, been able to choose Jessica. If chosen was the right word. Yet what other word was there?

He came up to her immediately, making her realize he'd been waiting for her. Pleased, she smiled up at him.

"I told Sage she and Donna could wander around by themselves," she said.

"Pretty safe here, even with the outsiders coming for the powwow," he told her.

"I watched you dance," she said as they went outside.

"I watched you, too."

What he didn't add was how it had made him feel to see his wife dancing with his sister, as caught up as any of the people in what she was doing. He'd noticed her lips moving and realized she must be chanting as well. Since she didn't know Paiute, she had to have found her own words. The depth of her involvement in the ceremony had touched his heart.

"I thought you looked magnificent," she said, surprising him speechless. "As Sage would say, this day has been awesome," she added. "I don't know when I've enjoyed myself more."

"It's not quite over," he told her. "There'll be food and music and good times yet to come."

"I already ate two buffalo tacos with Sage."

"She conned you into buying them, I bet."

"The poor kid was hungry."

He casually tucked her arm in his, elated when she didn't seem the least alarmed by the contact. "We'll take a stroll around while they get things started."

"I've never really gotten a good look at Pyramid Lake," she told him.

"You can't see much from here. I'll take you to the lake maybe next week. I have the feeling I promised Sage I'd volunteer for a Girl Scout cookout there about then.''

''And now you're volunteering me as well?''

''Looks like it.''

''No problem. You've already claimed the most expertise in outdoor cooking, so I get to watch.''

''No way. This is a cooperative venture. I demonstrate, you help the girls follow through.''

She made a face at him, wishing they could keep walking side by side forever, bantering back and forth, feeling close without any of the dangers of closeness.

By the time they turned back toward the community center, guitar music spilled out through the open doors and windows. Inside, couples had begun to dance.

Grandfather intercepted them as they entered. ''As the eldest Bearclaw male, I claim the honor of the first dance.'' He held his hand out to Laura.

She'd been preparing herself to tell Shane she didn't care to dance, but, somehow, she couldn't bring herself to refuse Grandfather.

He whirled her around the floor with considerable expertise, making her understand that it didn't matter if she lacked dancing experience with men—he had enough for both of them. Since she'd never been afraid of him, she wasn't now.

''I always pick the prettiest girl,'' Grandfather told her.

''Aren't you forgetting Jessica Patsona?'' she asked.

"Have to admit she's a looker," he said. "But so are you, in a different way."

"I wonder how many women you've charmed in your lifetime," she teased.

"More than he should have," Shane said, as he tapped Grandfather on the shoulder. "My turn now."

She was shifted into Shane's arms so quickly she didn't have time to protest, though that had been her intent. Laura stiffened initially, but when she found he had no intention of holding her any closer than Grandfather had, she began to relax, which made it easier to follow Shane's steps.

"I don't dance very much," she told him.

"We're doing pretty well together," he said.

It was true. As they glided over the floor, Laura began to feel as though she'd been doing this all her life. Fun! Why had she been so afraid to dance with a man?

Not that she was ready to let just any man put his arms around her like this. But she was safe with Shane. He'd told her so, and she believed him.

Soon, though, being in Shane's arms introduced emotions other than mere dancing pleasure. A tingling enveloped her, giving rise to an inexplicable urge to press her body closer to his. She felt flushed. Hot.

"It's warm in here," she murmured.

"Warm?" He sounded surprised, which flustered her.

"I need to cool off," she said bluntly.

''Probably do us both good,'' he agreed, and whirled her toward the door.

He led her off the floor with an arm around her waist and into the dusk outside. The moon was up, waxing toward full. She took a deep breath of desert air, where the leftover scents of the powwow mingled with the wilder smell of the vegetation and thought about moving away from Shane's encircling arm. But she didn't.

It felt right to her to be strolling along with him like this. For the first time in her life it felt right for her to be part of a couple.

Chapter Seven

The next morning, Laura rode out with Shane, feeling as though the evening before had been a dream. Had she really strolled in the moonlight with his arm around her? Had she actually hoped he might kiss her?

She shook her head. That wasn't like her at all.

"The day doesn't suit you?" Shane asked.

Laura glanced at him, perplexed.

"You frowned and shook your head," he told her. "Since I haven't said a word and the horses aren't misbehaving, I see nothing to be annoyed with except the day itself."

"It's a perfectly fine day," she admitted. Actually the morning was gorgeous, with a cool breeze not quite counteracting the warmth of the sun.

Looking across the sagebrush-covered land, she could see cottonwoods in the distance, telltale sentinels guarding the stream. "Are we going to camp by the water again?" she asked.

"I have a better plan. Your lame pinto mare looked to be near to foaling."

When he didn't go on, Laura nodded.

"You must know how mustang mares behave at that time," he added.

"I've read that they go off alone to bear their young."

"Right. And almost always in the same spot, year after year. I know where that might be. We'll check it out."

"How far?"

He waved a hand toward the northwest.

Which wasn't exactly pinpointing the location, but then this high desert terrain didn't have too many distinguishing landmarks—at least to her eyes.

"Isn't it dangerous for them to be by themselves when they give birth?" she asked.

"The mare's stuck in one place for the few hours it takes for the foaling and for the foal to get its traveling legs. The herd wouldn't wait around for her, so she'd be alone anyway. The places the mares choose are relatively safe. Coyotes are about the only predators around here. The big cats and the bears stay closer to the foothills."

A jackrabbit shot out from practically under the horses' hooves, but neither of them shied, and she commented on it.

He shrugged. "The good ones get used to desert wildlife early. Snakes'll spook 'em, but not rabbits or quail."

"I've never encountered a rattler," she said uneasily.

"You probably won't, either. Doesn't mean you might not see one. But snakes don't like close encounters any more than we do, so they generally take off if you give 'em the chance. Shy of men—like you."

Laura blinked, startled to hear herself compared to a rattler.

"Haven't noticed any other snake-like attributes yet, though," Shane said with a perfectly straight face.

He was teasing her, she realized belatedly. She wasn't used to being teased. She couldn't recall if her brother or her father might have done it before that dreadful Halloween, but they hadn't afterward.

In school she learned to be so successful at not being noticed that nobody there had bothered with her one way or the other. And she'd never before gotten close enough to a man so he felt free to tease. She rather enjoyed it.

"It might be worth it to shed my skin every year," she said. "That way I'd never look old." Though she was tempted to confront him about the "shy of men" comment, she didn't. After all, it was true.

"Be an interesting spectacle to watch, the skin shedding."

She decided not to touch that one. Changing the subject, she said, ''I enjoyed the dancing yesterday.''

''With me?''

''That, too,'' she admitted. ''But what I meant was the powwow dancing. It made me feel—oh, I don't know, I guess connected is the right word. Like I belonged.''

Shane, who'd always known he belonged, no matter what other problems he might have, didn't comment for a time. Their relationship was still so fragile he hesitated to say anything too personal that might make her retreat.

''That's one of the things a powwow's for, to remind us we're all part of a whole,'' he said finally.

Laura turned to him, smiling. ''Yes, that's exactly what I felt.''

Walking with her in the moonlight had certainly given him feelings that had nothing to do with the powwow. It had taken a ton of willpower not to go any further than putting an arm around her waist. She *was* his wife, and it was getting tougher every day to remember the ''in name only'' proviso.

''If the mare is foaling, won't we scare her if we get too close?'' she asked.

He smiled inwardly. Skittish was the word for her. Every time she got a little too close to him in body or conversation, she retreated to a safe distance or a safe topic.

''What I'm hoping to do is get us near her familiar place before she goes there,'' he said. ''Once we're camped upwind, we should be okay. And I'll put out a pan of water for her. In this dry country, that'll be a lure.''

He wished it were as simple to lure Laura closer.

Later, when they stopped to eat lunch by a stream, he pointed out the evidence that a herd had been there not long before them.

''The mare's herd?'' she asked.

''Can't be sure—but indications are it was a harem herd, not just that bunch of bachelors. This is the black stallion's territory, so it's probably his. Which means we may get lucky.''

They reached the foaling place in mid-afternoon, a depression between a couple of small hills. A few straggly cottonwoods grew at one end, showing water collected there in the wet season, though now it was as dry as a bleached bone.

''The trees'll offer cover for us,'' he said.

''Shade, too,'' she added. ''That sun is powerful.''

''We'll hold off on the tent until dark. If she shows up, the horses being nearby won't bother her, but the sight of a tent might.''

''I don't really need the tent,'' she told him. ''I can sleep outside as well as you can.''

After tending to the horses, Shane poured water into a shallow pan and set it at the edge of the nesting place. Retreating to their camp, partly screened by the trees, he helped her unroll the sleeping gear. They stretched out on their respective sleeping bags, side by side—though not too close—preparing to wait. Laura promptly fell asleep.

All that dancing getting to her, he thought. Her defenses down in sleep, she looked like the girl she'd once been, young and vulnerable, touching something protective within him.

Her energy and determination belied her air of fragility. Not that her body looked fragile. He couldn't think when he'd seen a woman's shape that appealed to him as much as hers did. Everything about her looked just right—breasts that would fit perfectly in his hands, those sweet curves to her hips....

Damn. He'd best do himself a favor and go back to thinking about being protective.

There was no question in his mind that she needed a man to watch out for her, and he was that man— because he knew how to deal with creatures who feared humans. Laura might look completely civilized on the surface, but her heart was as wild and wary as that of any mustang.

Last night she'd let him hold her while they danced. She hadn't sidled away from his arm around her waist afterward, either. Progress. If he could keep his own desire curbed, the next step would be for her to be able to tolerate a real kiss—not those featherweight ones she'd already accepted from him. No, not tolerate. Enjoy. She needed to learn to welcome his kiss. To want it.

He closed his eyes, imagining her in his arms, responding to his lovemaking, and drifted into a doze. He woke abruptly when one of their tethered horses snorted. Rolling cautiously onto his stomach, he raised his head enough to look through the trees.

A single mustang was headed their way. Frowning, he watched the slow approach of what he recognized as a pregnant mare. Her dusty coat was multicolored, so it must be Laura's lame pinto. Her dragging pace wasn't the slow of caution. This mare looked to be at the end of her rope. He didn't like the way her head hung down.

He reached across to Laura and touched her arm, saying in a low tone, "Wake up, but don't move. She's coming."

He felt her tense under his hand, but she stayed put.

"Okay, ease yourself onto your stomach so you can see," he told her.

"That's her," Laura said when she got into position. "But something's wrong with her. More than the lameness, I mean."

"'Fraid so."

"I have the vet pack with me, maybe I can help her."

"Don't move," he warned again. "Let her get where she wants to be."

His practiced eye told him the mare was, to all intents and purposes, beyond saving. She might not even have enough strength left to be able to push out the foal.

"She looks so pitiful," Laura mourned.

"She's dying." He spoke bluntly, wanting Laura

to know ahead of time what they'd be dealing with. "A wonder she made it here."

"I have medicine in the kit—"

"Too late."

She frowned at him. "We can at least try."

"The mare'll need help delivering her foal," he conceded, aware nothing was going to stop Laura. "Best to concentrate on that. Know anything about it?"

"Um, I've watched. If I have to, I think I can do what's necessary."

He heard the uncertainty in her voice, but he'd learned enough about Laura by now to know she wasn't likely to turn away from the sight of blood or to flinch at what had to be done, no matter what. He'd helped at enough births, so he was capable enough, but he thought Laura needed the chance to prove herself.

When the mare ignored the water, he knew she was beyond hope. She staggered into the depression and stood trembling, blood trickling from the opening of her birth canal.

"Already in labor," he muttered. "The foal's best chance to be born alive is to keep her on her feet— if we can. Time to go to her—move slowly and quietly."

When they joined her, other than a flicker of her ears, the mare ignored them, being too far gone to feel alarm. Shane spoke softly to her, telling her in Paiute that she was brave, that her baby would live and run in the wind as she'd done in her time.

"Before you die," he finished in English, "you will pass on the joy of being free to your child."

Tears pricked Laura's eyes at his words, but she blinked them away impatiently, concentrating on the birthing. The mare swayed on her feet as the foal's head popped into view. She stumbled, her legs giving way, and fell sideways just as the rest of her baby slipped out. Laura caught the foal, staggering under its weight as she eased it to the ground.

With the towel she'd brought, she wiped the membranes and fluid from the baby's face, then its body, noting absently that it was a male. The colt moved under her hands, already struggling to stand. A good sign, she knew.

"She's gone." Shane spoke from where he knelt beside the mare's head, his voice tinged with a sadness Laura understood and shared.

He straightened and came to look at the colt, who was black like his sire, marked only with one white patch on his forehead. He now stood uncertainly on all four legs, nuzzling at Laura.

"As the midwife, you get to name him," he told her, touched by her tenderness with the colt. "After all, he's yours to raise."

She was silent for a time, then said, "No, I'll let Sage choose his name."

"Why?" he asked.

Laura swallowed. "Because she'll be the one raising him."

"You don't want the problem?"

She turned to look at him, tears in her eyes. "Maybe that's it."

He put a hand on her shoulder. "No, it's not. You're giving him up, aren't you? Giving him to Sage. Why?"

She shrugged off his hand and snapped, "Stop questioning me. It's none of your business. I should think our first priority is to get this baby to the ranch before he starves to death."

Shane shrugged. "You're right." Gesturing at the pan of water, he added, "You might want to wash first."

Realizing for the first time she was covered with blood and fluid from the colt's birth process, Laura nodded and sluiced off what she could while Shane took care of fixing a sling for the colt so he could be tied onto the gelding for a ride back to the ranch.

When they arrived near dusk, Sage was so thrilled with her live present she could hardly speak. "He's mine?" she managed to squeak out. "I get to keep him?"

"Got to feed him every couple hours," Grandfather told her. "Best to start now. You'll be the only mother he knows."

"I'll get the calf bottle," Sage said, "and some milk."

Though warmed by Sage's obvious pleasure, Laura felt a certain heaviness in her heart. Doing her best to ignore it, she showered and changed. Though neither she nor Shane had eaten since noon, she felt she couldn't face the sight of food or bear anyone's company, so she left the house by the front door and turned to the right to be out of sight from the barn and corral. As she rounded the corner of the house she almost bumped into Shane.

"Figured you'd be coming this way," he said, as she drew back from him.

"Didn't it also occur to you that the reason might be I didn't want company?" she asked tartly.

"I knew that. Figured you needed it anyway. Besides, we've got unfinished business."

"None that I'm aware of." She knew if she stalked off, he'd follow her, so she stayed where she was. "Please leave me alone."

"Soon. Providing you're honest with me."

She stared up at him in the twilight, confused. "I don't understand what you mean."

"I want the truth. Since we're living in the same household and working together, what you do and how you act is my business. Just as if I really were your husband in every sense of the word. I should think you'd feel the same about me."

Laura thought over what he'd said. True, a marriage was about sharing, but theirs couldn't be called a real marriage.

"Whenever you get on your high horse with me, I know I've touched a raw spot," he continued. "Why are you afraid to tell me the real reason you gave Sage your colt?"

"I did it so she'd have something to take care of

and love." The words burst from Laura. "She needs to—"

"But *you* don't need anything to take care of and love, is that it?" His words beat at her, relentlessly.

Her first impulse was to pound his chest with her fists. With an effort she unclenched her hands, but she couldn't undo her anger. "You have no right..." she began.

"I'm taking the right. I know you're fond of horses. I saw how gentle and loving you were with the little colt."

Grasping the first thing that came to her, she said, "You know I won't be here long. It's better for him if he bonds with someone else."

"And better for you if you don't bond at all?"

Unable to control her anger, she raised her fisted hands. He caught her wrists. "Tell me," he demanded.

Furious as she was with him, she wasn't even slightly afraid. "It's not safe," she cried, hardly aware of what she was saying. "Not safe to get too fond of anybody or anything. Bad things happen."

Then to her horror, she burst into tears.

Shane put his arms around her, drawing her to him and she wept against his chest, tearing sobs that trembled through her.

"It's all right," he murmured, wondering if he'd gone too far with his probing. Her reluctance to be honest was to him like an abscess on a horse. Undrained, it made the animal sick, but lanced it healed.

Though lancing hurt, the abscess did, too, and was the more dangerous. Laura had some deep, ingrained hurt within her that would never heal unless he could persuade her to let him help.

As he stroked her back, speaking soothingly, it occurred to him that he was like the blind trying to lead the blind. Wasn't the truth of his reluctance to commit himself again to a woman in marriage because he feared exactly the same thing Laura did? That bad things happened if you got too fond of someone?

Not quite the same, he decided. He loved Sage unreservedly and was totally committed to her welfare. Who did Laura love in such a way? Did she feel that way about anyone?

Could she?

That was something he couldn't solve in one night. As her sobs eased, he coaxed her toward the front door, saying, "Come eat with me. I hate to eat alone. There's leftover chicken from supper—we'll have that."

Leading her into the kitchen, he urged her into a chair and set a tissue box on the table in front of her. "Since you were entitled to an outdoor meal that you didn't get this evening," he said, "I'll do the honors."

Sage chose that moment to bounce into the kitchen, full of chatter about her colt. "I'm going to call him Star on account of the white mark on his head. It actually does look like a star. Grandfather says he can tell Star'll be a good, sound horse when he grows up. I'm getting him an old blanket to sleep on, okay?''

She barely waited for Shane's nod of agreement before dashing off. But she'd been there long enough for Laura to make the effort to compose herself and, when Shane set food in front of her, she ate a little.

Later, in bed, Laura tried to sort out her feelings. Her anger at Shane had been washed away by her tears and, yes, by the way he held and comforted her. She didn't regret what she'd admitted. Why regret telling the truth? Even if it had been forced out of her.

In any case, the little colt was far better off with Sage. They could grow up together.

Laura sighed and turned over. She'd miss seeing it happen, seeing Sage turn into a young woman and Star into the good, sound horse Grandfather had predicted he'd become. She'd miss Grandfather, too.

And Shane? That didn't bear thinking about. Not tonight.

But she would have to think about it sometime because they would be parting soon. Not for good, she needed to stay around long enough to make sure Sage's future was secure. Once she was through studying the two herds on reservation land, though, she'd move on to the next group of mustangs.

Though there were other herds she needed to research in Northern Nevada, she told herself that maybe she ought to choose another state next. Montana. It was best for everyone that she leave Nevada for a while. Sage had to get used to her coming and going.

And I need to get away from Shane, she admitted to herself.

He was fast becoming a friend, and she could use a friend—couldn't everyone? If that were all, there'd be no problem. But being with him was stirring emotions she didn't know she had, triggering feelings she thought she'd long ago eliminated. Plus introducing some new and alarming sensations she didn't dare explore, much as she longed to.

Yes, it was best to head for Montana the minute she finished up with the herds here. To stay on much longer was too risky. She didn't worry so much about what Shane might do—it was herself she feared. What might happen if she let herself get out of control?

The mere thought alarmed her.

Chapter Eight

While they were eating breakfast the next morning, the phone rang. Sage jumped up to answer it, then called, "Grandfather, it's for you."

When she came back to the table she looked so downcast that Laura asked her what was the matter.

"You're going to hate me," Sage told her.

"I doubt that very much," Laura said.

"And Shane's going to be mad at me," Sage added.

"You might be right," he said. "More so if you go on hedging and don't get to the point."

Sage looked even more distressed. "I just remembered I took two phone messages yesterday and forgot to tell either of you about them. I'm sorry, but I got so excited about Star and all."

Shane set down his coffee mug and fixed his gaze on his sister. "What messages?"

"Yours was from the Outpost saying they sold the last carving and when could you get more to them. I told them you'd call." Sage took a deep breath. "Laura's was from her brother. He wanted her to call him back."

"No harm done," Laura said. "I'll call him today." Noticing Grandfather come into the kitchen, she rose. "Right now, in fact. It's early, maybe I can catch him before he goes to the clinic."

As she walked to the phone, she wondered what Nathan wanted. She wasn't sure she was ready to see him again so soon after their last encounter. Maybe Jade had talked him into a more reasonable frame of mind, though. She hoped so.

Nathan picked up the phone on the second ring. "Oh, hi, sis," he said. "Jade and I would like to have you and Shane over for dessert and coffee Friday evening. How's that for you?"

"This Friday?" she asked. Only two days away.

"You got it."

Deciding there was no point in putting him off, since then he might think something was wrong, she said, "It sounds okay, but let me check with Shane."

"Great. You can let Jade know."

Laura walked back to the table where Shane now sat alone. "Nathan and Jade have invited us for Friday evening dessert," she told him. "What do you think?"

"No problem here." He gave her an assessing look. "Do you want to go?"

She shrugged, trying to behave as though it didn't matter one way or the other. "I suppose we should."

"Okay, we'll come back early enough on Friday to make the drive over to Tourmaline." He shoved his chair back and stood. "I'll leave a message on the Outpost's answering machine, and then we'll ride."

They were planning to camp for several consecutive nights near the usual watering spots along the stream so she could get a close look at the mustangs in the two herds. Once she finished doing that, she'd have the reservation mustangs tallied and could go on to the next site. Which she'd already decided would be Montana.

As they headed out with a pack horse carrying extra gear, Laura wondered again if it might have been wiser to postpone another meeting with her brother until she returned from Montana. But, since she'd already called Jade back to accept, it was too late.

"I get the feeling you're afraid to visit your brother," Shane said after a while.

"No, not exactly. It's just that I'd have liked a longer time span so he could get more adjusted to the idea of me being married. I don't want any more confrontations."

"Being offered dessert sounds more like a peace offering. In the old days, once a stranger was offered food in a lodge of my people, he knew he was safe from harm.''

Perhaps Shane was right, and her worry was for nothing. She decided not to think about it anymore. The morning was as beautiful as only a Nevada high desert June day could be. She was riding with a man she trusted, a man who was her friend. No one could ask for a better companion. And she enjoyed what she was doing—so much more satisfying than sitting in an office back east.

Shane, watching Laura's frown disappear and her shoulders straighten, smiled, pleased to have banished what was troubling her. To him, Nathan hadn't seemed like the type of man to carry a grudge. If it weren't for the marriage agreement he and Laura had made, he'd have no qualms about visiting the Walkers. As it was though, since she hadn't fully explained the situation to her brother, he felt uneasy. The way she'd put things made it sound like theirs might be a real marriage.

Apparently he hadn't inherited Grandfather's deviousness, because he much preferred everything laid out in plain sight.

Dismissing the future visit, he concentrated on looking for mustang sign. He already knew where he'd like to camp—providing the horses cooperated and didn't hare off on some unexpected tangent.

''Jessica is one of the most attractive women I've ever met,'' Laura said unexpectedly.

He smiled one-sidedly. ''You'd get no argument from any male on the res.''

"Including you?"

He shrugged. "I'm not blind. Why do you ask?"

"No reason."

Ha. Women never brought up another woman's name for no reason. "Still wondering why I didn't marry her?" he asked.

She shot him an indignant look, and then turned her head away from him, but not before he saw her telltale blush.

"Told you I didn't intend to marry," he said. "No more than the truth. If you want my opinion of Jessica, I doubt marriage has ever been her primary concern. She's had plenty of chances."

He let that settle a while and then added, "'Course, now that I've taken the plunge, I have to admit maybe I was wrong about wedded bliss."

That brought her accusing gaze back to him. "You're teasing me."

He grinned. Laura was different from any woman he'd ever gotten to know well. Her reactions fascinated him. "Just trying to make up for lost time," he said. "You don't strike me as a gal who ever got teased much."

"I'm none too sure I care for it."

A guy had to spell everything out for this woman. "If I didn't like you, I wouldn't tease you."

She smiled at him. "Actually, I don't mind."

"That I tease you or that I like you?"

"Either. Both. I was just thinking I've never had a male friend before."

Trying to keep him in his place was she? He

thought of the night camp to come, with a moon close to full and wondered if he was going to be able to keep his hands off her. Probably not. Scratch the probably.

Past noon, after they'd stopped to eat and rest the horses, they were on their way again. Shane saw mustang sign. The herd was traveling in the right direction—he'd chosen the perfect spot to camp. Since the wild horses were ahead of them, he figured they'd cross the stream, but come back to drink at their customary spot before nightfall.

If he and Laura camped on this side of the stream among the cottonwoods, but without putting up a tent, they wouldn't spook the herd. She should be able to get a good look at every horse in the black stallion's harem and some idea of how healthy each was.

Later, at the campsite, as they were unpacking gear, she said, "No tent?"

"We're taking a chance if we set it up before the herd comes back," he told her. "After they leave, we can put up the tent for you."

She shook her head. "I haven't slept under the stars since I was a kid at summer camp. I'm looking forward to doing just that tonight."

"We'll be sleeping under the moon as well," he added.

"In the old days people used to believe that if you let the moon's rays strike you while asleep, you'd wake crazy—a lunatic," Laura said.

"Interesting concept. Think it'll happen to us?"

She made a face at him and he grinned, at the same time thinking that there really was something about a full or nearly full moon that did promote lovemaking. It was certainly on his mind, and the moon hadn't even risen yet.

Laura tried not to think about lying on her sleeping bag gazing up at the moon with Shane next to her. A romantic idyll. If she believed in such things—which she didn't. Romance had no place in her life. But more and more, Shane did.

She marveled at the effortless way he handled the horses, seeming to communicate with them mind to mind. He moved so fluidly, one motion flowing into another. When he sat down with his back to a tree, took out a knife and began to whittle, she watched with interest to see what would come out of the length of willow branch he'd cut.

His artisan's hands were strong and capable. She liked the feel of them when he touched her. In fact, she wouldn't mind if he were touching her right this minute. If she felt that way now, how was it going to be under the moon? Would he kiss her goodnight? Would it be one of those quickie kisses, or what Sage called a real kiss?

Stop fantasizing, she warned herself. You don't want or need anything from him but friendship. But she could do nothing to blunt her acute awareness of him, though she managed to stay where she was instead of wandering over to sit next to him the way she wanted to.

Just before dusk, on the other side of the stream,

the black stallion and his harem of mares ambled cautiously up to the water. Crouched low, Laura scribbled in her notebook, totting up the color and condition of each mare, then the stallion.

When she finished, so had the horses, and she watched them trot off, manes and tails blowing in the evening breeze, a perfect picture of freedom.

"Beautiful," she murmured, shifting to sit on her sleeping bag. Since they'd be sleeping in their clothes, all she removed were her boots.

Beside her Shane nodded.

Shaking off the spell cast by the mustangs, she said, "I noticed quite a few scars marring the stallion's coat."

"Bite and hoof marks from challenges. He has to fight other stallions to keep his harem."

"I knew about the challenges, but I never realized the stallions actually got hurt."

"Wait'll you see one. Lady, these are *wild* horses. No holds barred, in love or war."

"I know harems are the norm, but I've sometimes thought it's unfair the mares don't get to choose the stallion they'd prefer."

Shane shrugged. "As long as their stallion is victorious in all his battles, he's the pick of the crop, isn't he?"

True. She glanced at him, noting the wide shoulders and his powerful build. The thought crossed her mind that Shane was likely to be the victor in any fight with another man. The pick of the crop.

Shane put away his knife, brushed the wood shavings from his jeans, rose and ambled over to sit cross-legged on his sleeping bag. He put what he'd carved to his lips, blowing into it, coaxing a melody from what she realized now was a wooden flute. How clever he was.

"What's that tune?" she asked

He paused long enough to say, "I'm making one up—the way a man is supposed to when he woos a fair maiden with his love flute."

A thrill tingled through her at his words. She listened to the plaintive notes, feeling them infuse her with warmth, enjoying the wooing.

The moon chose that moment to become visible through the branches of the cottonwoods. In silence they watched it rise higher, casting silver light over all. Sighing, Laura lay back and stared up at the moon. Moon madness. Moon magic. She'd best be careful not to let those silvery rays lure her into behavior she'd regret—never mind how much she yearned to touch him.

Shane stopped playing and eased down onto his sleeping bag. Raising onto one elbow, he looked down at Laura, radiant in the moonlight. She glanced at him, their gazes crossed, caught and held. He heard her catch her breath. Slowly, slowly, her hand came up to his cheek.

"Shane?" His name was no more than a whisper.

He bent his head, his lips finding hers, meaning to hold himself in check. But once he tasted the sweetness of her mouth he was lost. The next he knew, he held her tightly, the kiss deep and demanding.

As he reached for control, he realized her arms had come up to hold him to her and her lips, under his, returned his kiss. Trying to curb the heat that shot through him at the realization she was responding, he coaxed her lips apart, catching her sigh in his mouth.

He needed more, needed to touch her, to caress her, to feel the softness of her breasts under his hands. The buttons on her shirt opened under his fingers, and she drew in her breath when his hand covered her breast.

But then she pulled away from him, averting her face while she fumbled with the buttons of her shirt.

He'd moved too fast, he decided, and sighed. It looked to be a long night ahead.

When she had her shirt closed again, he said, "Scared?"

"I—no. But—"

Tiring of waiting for the rest, he asked, "But you didn't enjoy what we were doing?"

"I don't think I want to answer that," she said.

Aha. She *had* enjoyed it and didn't want to lie. "Then why stop?"

"Because I—you—" Again she paused, finally blurting, "Stop asking questions!"

"Either you don't want to tell me or you don't know," he said.

No answer.

Shane gave up and lay back on his sleeping bag, looking up at the stars.

"Why must you always probe?" she asked after a time.

"Because I need to know how you feel, what makes you tick. It's like when I pick up a piece of wood for carving. I can't see right away what's hiding inside the wood. I need to look at and touch it many times before what lives in there lets me know what kind of animal it is."

"What's that have to do with me?"

"I can't see what's hiding inside you, either. I want to, but you won't let me."

"Maybe that's because I don't care to be carved into what you perceive me to be."

He turned his head to look at her. "No, you'd rather hide. But do you understand I don't carve what I want to from the wood? The result would be faulty. It's becoming aware of what that piece of wood can be that makes any carving successful. I'm not trying to force you into anything."

After a long silence, she said, "You're right. It's always easier to blame someone else. The problem is mine, not yours."

He waited, hoping she'd go on to rid herself of what troubled her, but when she spoke, she changed the subject, running away again.

"Have the Paiutes always lived on this land?"

"If you're asking were my people—the Numa—displaced, yes and no. Like all the early tribes, they were nomadic, living part of the year in one place and part in another. But Pyramid Lake *was* one of the places."

"It must feel to you as though you belong here."

What was she getting at? "I've always felt that way, yes. As much because of the people around me as the land, though."

"I don't belong anywhere." She spoke flatly. "Sometimes I think I never will."

He couldn't assure her the time would come when she would because he felt she had to let go of what troubled her before she'd be ready to find her place.

Before he could come up with anything positive, she said, "Good night, Shane," and turned her back to him.

He'd been right. It turned out to be a very long night.

After taking forever to fall asleep, Laura woke when the sky began to lighten. When she saw Shane not only wasn't in his sleeping bag next to her, but that the bag itself was gone, she sat up and looked around. Reassured by the tempting odor of coffee that he hadn't completely deserted her, she stood up, ran her fingers through her hair and picked up her boots.

With any luck they'd find the bachelor herd today and she'd be able to tally them so she wouldn't be facing another night camp with Shane beside her, near enough to touch if she reached out. If only he knew how hard it had been for her to turn away from what he offered last night.

Tonight the moon would be even brighter, but the moonlight wasn't to blame. What she felt came from deep within her, a demand that she wasn't sure she'd be able to deny much longer. She'd never expected to be gripped by such a need. Of course she knew what it was. Physical attraction. Shane had more allure than any man should be allowed to possess, and she wasn't allure-proof, not where he was concerned.

Later, when they were mounted and riding side by side, she said, "Do you think we'll spot the bachelors today?"

He shrugged. "Even though I know their habits, with mustangs it's a crapshoot—you never know if they'll really show up where you expect them to."

By mid-afternoon, when Shane hadn't spotted any sign of the smaller herd, Laura told herself if it was a crapshoot, then this wasn't her lucky day. It looked very much like another night's camp was in the offing.

Once again, he chose a spot by the stream, early enough so the two of them could wade in the water before there was any chance of the mustangs coming for their evening drink. She watched enviously as Shane shucked off his shirt and splashed water onto his bare chest and shoulders.

"You can do the same," he told her. "I won't watch if you don't want me to."

The thought of him watching her strip to the waist brought back the feeling of his hand cupping her breast. An image rose in her mind of him catching her in his arms, her naked breasts pressed against his bare skin. How would that feel? She didn't know, but she realized with dismay how desperately she wanted to find out.

Because she wore a T-shirt underneath, she finally took off her long-sleeved shirt and splashed water onto her arms, telling herself firmly it would be madness to get any more involved with Shane than she already was.

Dusk came and went without any mustangs appearing. Inevitably, the moon rose, drenching them with silver light. Shane stretched out on his sleeping bag and closed his eyes. She watched him warily, denying her disappointment there was to be no love music tonight.

He was more or less making it obvious if anything happened, it wouldn't be at his instigation. He certainly couldn't expect it to be at hers, so maybe the truth was he just didn't care one way or the other.

Still sitting up on her bag, she scowled down at him. He hadn't even said good-night. Plopping down onto her bag, she told herself it didn't matter.

"I take it we aren't going to feel the earth move?" he said.

Confused, she said, "What?"

He opened his eyes, turning his head to look at her. "Not a Hemingway fan?"

She didn't have a clue what he meant.

Apparently her expression told him that, because he gave her a half-smile. "Let's hope the time comes when I can explain that, and you'll know what I mean.''

From somewhere in the distance a coyote began singing to the moon. "Reminding us the Trickster is keeping an eye on us," he said.

"Hemingway and the Trickster are not in my ballpark.''

"All Native American cultures have Tricksters to remind us that when you think you have the world by the tail, it turns out to be Trickster's tail. He jerks it away, and the joke's on you.''

"I understand the concept, but not your usage.''

"Take us," he said. "Here we are under *muha patseponia*—a full moon—and what are we doing? Listening to the coyotes, that's what.''

As she understood the meaning behind what he was saying, her breath caught. He wanted to do exactly what he'd done last night. Exactly what she wanted him to do.

Because she knew what the consequences would be, she had to swallow twice before she could get the words out. "Well, you *could* kiss me goodnight.''

For a long moment he didn't move, and then suddenly she was in his arms, his lips on hers, the kiss both coaxing and demanding, luring her farther into desire, into the need for more.

He hadn't replaced his shirt and she could feel the ripple of his back muscles under his smooth bare skin, reminding her of how powerful he was. Instead of feeling fear, it excited her. He didn't frighten her because she trusted him, knowing he'd never harm her. He could, but he wouldn't. Not Shane.

As his hands slipped under her T-shirt to caress her breasts, she ceased to think clearly, trapped within the web of passion he evoked, only able to feel an increasingly wild abandon.

Everything except Shane became unreal. There was no time, no place, just the two of them. She longed to stay here forever but the need rising in her made her want more.

She had no idea of how or when they both lost their clothes, but she was exquisitely aware of the wonder of his skin against hers. His touch was gentle but arousing as he caressed her everywhere so that she melted inside.

And then he joined with her, giving her what she hadn't known she wanted, taking her with him into a place she'd never been, one she hadn't dreamed existed.

As Shane held her afterward, he realized, as he'd half-expected, she'd been a virgin. He'd violated the agreement he'd signed, but it had certainly been with her encouragement and cooperation, no doubt about that.

''Shane?'' she murmured after a time.

''Hmm?''

''I told you the moon was dangerous.''

He chuckled, tightening his hold. ''So it is. Are you sorry?''

''No. Yes. Oh, I don't know.'' She snuggled

against him. "How can I answer that when I'm not even sure how it happened. Or if it should have."

"You have to admit it was perfectly legal."

"But I didn't mean for us to—" She bogged down.

"Make love? That's what husbands and wives do."

"Yes, but not us. This isn't a real marriage."

Her words cut into him like a knife, making him release her and sit up. "If it isn't, just what the hell do you think it is?" he growled.

She sat up, too, grabbing her shirt to cover her bare breasts. "We made an agreement—"

"Which we've already violated."

"I don't mean that paper I made you sign. We agreed that once you retained custody of Sage, we'd be free to go our separate ways."

Though the night was still warm, Shane felt as though he was encased in ice. "That's wrong." His words were involuntary. "You wanted this as much as I did."

She bit her lip. "I couldn't help it. Being with you like this—" She paused. "Actually I didn't know I was capable of lust," she finished.

"Lust," he repeated, wondering if that's all it had been. He wasn't sure, and he realized he didn't care to explore the possibility it might have been something else. Something more.

One thing he did know. If she thought she was going to get away from him easily, she was damn well mistaken.

Chapter Nine

Riding back to the house the next morning, Laura was too preoccupied with what had happened the night before to try to start a conversation. Whether Shane felt the same or not, she didn't know, but he, too, rode in silence.

She couldn't bring herself to admit it was a mistake she wouldn't make again, because that would be a lie. The truth was she was more aware of him than ever and in a different way. Back East, her women co-workers had sighed over how sexy certain men were, going into what she'd felt was unnecessary detail about certain outstanding physical characteristics. She'd never understood why, but she did now.

Shane was a magnificent male specimen in the

same way the black stallion was. That didn't mean, though, that she intended to allow their relationship to deepen. What if she got so involved she couldn't bear to leave? She might no longer be afraid of him, but what could happen to her was scary. Experience had taught her it didn't pay to grow too fond of anything or anybody.

And yet she wanted him to hold her again, to kiss her. She wanted to make love with him. A sigh welled up from her heart. How had she gotten herself into this anyway?

When she glanced at Shane, she saw he was frowning—actually more of a scowl. Not at her or at anything she could see ahead, so it must be at his thoughts. Was he regretting the night? She wished she knew.

To get relief from going over and over the same thing in her mind, she groped for something to say and fastened on where they'd be going later today. "Did I ever tell you how my brother and his wife came to adopt Tim?" she asked.

"You didn't even tell me about your brother until shortly before he showed up," Shane retorted, sounding definitely grumpy.

Deciding to skip over that omission, she said, "Nathan and Jade actually met each other and Tim at the same time." She went on to describe the car accident Tim had been in and the circumstances that had forced her brother and his not-then-wife together as they tried to take care of the little boy who wouldn't tell them who he was.

"You're saying you don't think the two of them would have married if it hadn't been for Tim?" Shane asked.

She nodded. "I don't mean they married so they could adopt him, but the forced togetherness made them realize they were—well, I suppose you might say meant for each other."

He slanted her a look. "Do you believe they were?"

"I think so, yes. My brother was involved in a disastrous marriage—his ex-wife was impossible— so he'd made up his mind never to walk down the aisle again. Jade's nothing like that horrible woman."

"Meant for each other," he repeated. "Easy to say."

"For them it was true," she said defensively.

"So it follows the same must be true for others?"

She glared at him. "I don't know! Why must you always back me into a corner?"

He gestured at the sagebrush-covered land around them. "Not a corner in sight. Why do you always retreat and shut yourself off? You said you weren't afraid of me."

"I'm not afraid of you!" Her voice rose. "I just want to be left alone."

Shane decided to back off. If she got any more upset, the visit with the Walkers might prove even more awkward than he suspected it might be. Last night she'd given him a part of herself, an experience he'd remember all his life. But what about the hidden rest of her?

Probing didn't work. Companionship didn't, either. Not even lovemaking, great though that had been. She guarded whatever secret that made her so fearful as though it were more valuable than Fort Knox gold.

He wondered if her brother might have a clue. Even if Nathan did, though, he wouldn't be about to reveal anything to a man he figured had conned his sister into getting married.

As for the lovemaking—Shane smiled at the memory of her passion, both surprising and infinitely arousing. Yet afterward, she'd retreated from him as fast as she could backpedal.

"I'm looking forward to meeting Tim," he said, as neutral a statement as he could come up with and fairly truthful. He'd already met her brother and, though he hoped their relationship would become more cordial, he wasn't laying any bets.

"I wish we could bring Grandfather along this evening," she said.

He raised his eyebrows. "Why?"

"Oh, I don't know. Maybe because he has a way of saying things that makes everyone stop and think."

"Wait until he starts telling you ancient Paiute legends. Sometimes the point is so obscure even I have trouble locating it. And I grew up on the stories."

"Maybe that's on purpose—to make you keep trying to find the meaning."

Shane shrugged. "He's a devious old man. Medicine men are always devious. It makes me wonder if I'll ever master all I need to know to become one."

"I like your Grandfather."

"Just remember you can't always take at face value what he seems to be saying. He doesn't lie, but his way of thinking can be as twisting as a snake track."

"I'll bet he's right most of time, though."

"You got it," Shane said. "Frustrates the hell out of me sometimes."

The sun was lowering when they rode into the corral. Nobody came to meet them, so they took care of the horses before going inside the house. Something good was cooking in the Crock-Pot—chili by the spicy smell—but no one was around.

"Sage is probably out in the barn doing her best to spoil that colt," Shane said. "Wouldn't surprise me if Grandfather isn't egging her on."

"Babies need a lot of attention," she reminded him. "I'm for a shower and change of clothes."

"Sounds good to me. Want to shower with a friend and save water?"

She frowned at him, but her flush told him he'd made her imagine them naked together with the water sluicing down. Something he'd better stop thinking about right now or suffer the consequences.

* * *

After supper—both of them duded up some—they left Sage and Grandfather to the dishes and set off for Tourmaline. Laura wore a pink dress with a full skirt that made her look like a rose to him. She smelled good, too.

He was tempted to tell her how much he wanted her, here and now, but didn't, considering what lay ahead. The visit might turn out to be okay, but he wasn't looking forward to it.

Laura did her best to keep her gaze from returning again and again to Shane. He wore his turquoise bolo with a Western-style tan shirt and jeans, and she thought he was the most gorgeous thing on two feet. She found it difficult to keep from touching him, which unsettled her considerably. Just what she needed, considering the ordeal ahead.

Jade wouldn't be a problem, but Nathan was another story. She knew he wasn't satisfied with her reason for marrying, despite her claim that she liked Shane and they got along well together. Too well, if last night was any indication. Just the thought of it sent a little quiver of desire running through her.

Enough of that!

Thank heaven it would be early enough for Tim to still be up. She hoped the boy would provide some distraction.

When they arrived at the Walkers' old Victorian home, Nathan was out on a call. Laura was surprised to find they weren't the only guests. Her assumption that they would be had been wrong. Uncertain whether she really wanted strangers present, she summoned a smile for an older woman and a man who looked to be about Nathan's age.

Jade made the introductions. "Gert," she added, "is an old friend of Nathan's. And David is her nephew, here for a visit."

Gert Severin, a pleasant-faced woman of about sixty, nodded, saying, "David may turn out to be a sojourner rather than a visitor. An interesting term, don't you think? A visit always sounds like popping in and out of a place, while a sojourn implies a leisurely stay."

Following Gert's lead, the conversation remained casual while Jade served coffee and dessert. At this point Nathan returned with little Tim, who'd gone along for the ride, and they all sat down to eat together.

Tim, sitting next to Laura, said, "Gert's my friend. At first I didn't think she would be, but she is. I got lots of friends here."

"Friends are good to have," Gert told him.

"Some of them," David muttered, then shook his head. "Sorry. Spoke out of turn."

As soon as they finished and returned to the living room, David thanked Jade, excused himself and left the house.

"He'll adjust," Gert said. "It takes time." She didn't go on to explain.

Nathan and Jade both nodded, so apparently they knew whatever it was that David had to adjust to. Since it wasn't really any of her business, Laura was just as glad not to know. She had enough problems of her own.

"You don't smile very much," Tim told her, plopping down on the footstool near the couch where she and Shane were sitting.

She managed to smile at him, but he looked dubious, as though he knew the smile wasn't from her heart. Getting up, he left the room.

Feeling Shane's hand reach for hers, she tightened her fingers around his, some of her tension easing.

"Much as I hate to eat and run," Gert said, glancing at her watch, "I have someone coming who couldn't get here earlier—so duty calls." Fixing her gaze on Laura, she added, "I'm glad I had the chance to meet you—and your husband."

Laura exchanged a look with Shane as Gert left. Did he feel, as she did, that there was something odd about this setup?

"Is Gert one of your colleagues?" she asked her brother.

"One of my favorites," he said.

Tim returned, carrying a stuffed green frog, which he dropped onto Laura's lap. "You hold Freddie," he told her. "Freddie'll make you feel better."

Taken totally unaware, Laura couldn't control her sudden spate of tears. Feeling Shane's arm come around her, she turned her head into his chest.

"Whatever it is," he murmured into her ear, "I'm here."

As from a distance, she heard Jade say, "I don't think Laura needs Freddie anymore, Tim. She has

Shane now, you see, just like you have Daddy and me.''

"Okay," Tim said.

When Laura composed herself enough to face everyone, Tim and the frog had disappeared. Jade held out her hand, saying, "Let's go freshen up."

Laura followed Jade from the room, leaving Nathan and Shane alone together. When she finished washing her face, running a brush through her hair and applying new lipstick, Jade was waiting in the upstairs hall beside an open door. Inside the room, Laura glimpsed a crib.

Aware that her sister-in-law had had a previous miscarriage, involuntarily Laura glanced at Jade's waistline.

Jade's smile was a bit sad. "Four months along," she confirmed. "We pray I can carry this one to term."

"I'll pray right along with you," Laura told her.

"Thanks. We're optimistic." She laid a hand on Laura's arm. "Tim didn't mean to upset you."

"It was sweet of him to offer to let me hold Freddie, but it did take me by surprise."

"I think you've chosen a good man, for whatever reason. Don't let him go."

Realizing Jade understood the marriage hadn't been a love match, Laura was tempted to confide in her, to ask her what she ought to do now, but she held back. Whatever was between her and Shane was their secret and no one else's.

As they went down the stairs to the living room,

Jade's words thrummed in Laura's head. *Don't let him go.* Isn't that exactly what she intended to do?

Just before they reached the bottom, Jade stopped her, leaning over to whisper, "Please don't be angry with Nathan because he asked Gert over. He was worried about you, that's all."

Confused about why Jade thought she'd be angry, Laura murmured, "No problem."

When they entered the living room, Nathan was saying, "That's some hatchery you've got going at Pyramid. It was past time someone took the initiative about preserving cutthroat trout."

"Come out and I'll take you fishing," Shane told him.

Nathan nodded, looking up at Laura. "Okay now, sis?"

"Freddie undid me for a minute, that's all," she said. "I'm fine. But you have to understand we've been camping out with the mustangs for two days. We barely got back in time to come over here, so all I'm really up for at the moment is sacking out. Which is probably why I overreacted."

Shane crossed to stand next to her and, without thinking what she was doing, she leaned against him.

"I think we'd better bid these two good-night before they fall asleep on their feet," Jade said to Nathan.

He nodded and, at the door, gave Laura a hug before shaking Shane's hand. "See you soon," he said.

As they started home, Laura leaned her head back against the seat and sighed. "What a strange evening," she said.

"Want to tell me about Freddie?" he asked.

Laura took a moment to gather her thoughts. "He used to be my frog before I gave him to Nathan. Then when Nathan gave him to Tim, the frog turned out to be Tim's security blanket. Tim knows Freddie belonged to me first, and so I guess he thought he ought to give me a chance to hold him."

"In case you needed a security blanket."

"I suppose."

"He's an observant little boy. Did you give the frog to your brother for the same reason you gave the colt to Sage? Because you didn't want to get too attached to Freddie?"

Laura thought about it. "I must have," she said at last. "Freddie used to be my favorite stuffed animal."

"Something must have caused you to be so afraid of getting too fond of anything."

She tensed. Because he hadn't phrased it as a question, she didn't have to answer. Wasn't going to answer. Her long-ago therapist had probed in this same general area, though she hadn't known about Freddie the Frog. Nothing had come of it.

Therapist. Now why did that word ring a bell? She sat straight up as the connection struck her, crying, "She's a shrink!"

Shane turned to look at her. "Who is?"

"Gert Severin. I just remembered they took Tim

to a shrink named Dr. Severin a couple of times. That's why she was there tonight. To evaluate me. That sneaky brother of mine—how could he?''

''Since Gert missed the scene with Freddie, I'd say she found you fairly normal.''

She glared at him. ''That's not the point. I think Nathan was completely out of bounds to do such a thing. I'm furious with him.''

''He's worried about you.''

''That's what Jade said. But I didn't understand at the time what she was getting at. I could wring his neck. For starters.''

''I think Nate's all but convinced he can stop worrying,'' Shane said.

''Nate?''

He shrugged. ''Told me to call him that. I figure if he's accepted me, that means he thinks our marriage might be okay.''

Since her brother would never have dropped in the Nate business if he were still suspicious of Shane, Laura had to concede the point. On the other hand, she hadn't told Nathan the complete truth—she'd added that darn embroidery.

''Could be he thinks we're meant for each other,'' Shane said.

About to react, she realized he was teasing her. Two could play at that. ''Have you considered he might be right?'' she asked airily.

''Sure.''

Taken completely aback, she stared at him.

''Considered it, that is,'' he added. ''Have you?''

Still teasing, was he? She'd fix him. "Actually, no. You probably were made for someone like, let's say Jessica."

He swerved the truck onto the shoulder, shut off the motor, unbuckled both their seat belts and pulled her into his arms. His face was so close she felt she was breathing in the air he exhaled, so intimate an exchange that a thrill ran through her.

"So why do I want to kiss you instead?" he growled just before their lips met.

If she'd had the slightest thought of not allowing herself to get carried away by his touch, she lost it in the kiss as her very bones melted.

She wanted to stay where she was forever, held close to him as she met the demand in his kiss with her own. She relished the taste of him—the slight hint of chocolate from Jade's dessert mingling with his own distinct flavor, one she knew she'd never forget.

His scent surrounded her, clean and masculine, infinitely arousing. Shane was rapidly changing the old familiar Laura into a passion-driven stranger she hardly recognized—scary for someone who'd always prided herself on her control.

When he released her she sighed, not wanting the closeness to end.

"Buckle up," he told her as he started the truck. "Remember, you got an aggressive driver behind the wheel. We Bearclaws don't like to lose."

"I'll bet you don't lose very often," she replied.

He shot her a quick glance. "Keep that in mind."

However he felt about this woman he'd so un-expectedly married, Shane thought, he damn well wasn't about to lose her. No matter what.

He'd never been one to sort through his feelings, trying to figure out how he felt about things. Up until now, he'd always known. But Laura's arrival in his life had changed that. All he was sure of with her was that he didn't mean to let go.

"Don't be too hard on your brother," he said after a time. "For all he knew about me I might have been Godzilla in disguise."

"He should have had the sense to realize I wouldn't have married Godzilla," she retorted. "Inviting a shrink to check me—or you—out is the limit."

"My take is he wanted *us* checked out rather than you or me."

"You mean how we related to each other? Big deal. We could have put on a perfect partners act and how would Gert have known?"

"Are you trying to hint that we aren't perfect partners?" he teased.

"Be serious. I think Nathan was way out of line. No wonder Jade apologized, though I didn't understand what for at the time."

"I liked Gert. Learned a new word. That's what my people used to be in the old days—sojourners."

"I don't blame *her*. Doctors stick together—she was doing Nathan a favor."

"No favor to haul that nephew of hers into a bunch of strangers."

"Who? Oh, David. Yes, he did seem upset about something." Laura paused, then added, "But no more than I would have been if I'd known what my brother was up to."

"Sleep on it. Grandfather recommends two nights." He refrained from pointing out that she wasn't facing the different turn their marriage had taken, either, and that might be contributing to her being upset. But he didn't intend to push—it was her call.

What he really wanted to know was whether she meant to share his bed now. Asking wasn't an option. Either she would or she wouldn't.

"The moon still looks full tonight," he said, spotting its pale yellow circle rising over the hills.

She turned her head to look through the side window. "Why is it the moon always looks bigger in Nevada?"

"It probably doesn't in Las Vegas."

"With all that neon they might not even know the moon is there. But I meant here in Northern Nevada. You can see everything better here."

Shane wondered if that was true where they were concerned.

As if reading his mind, she added. "Take me, for example. I'm not the same person you rescued the day we met. And I want you to know it's not easy to change."

"Might not be, but I sure am enjoying it."

Laura blinked. "You're changing, too?" she asked.

"Some," he admitted. "Not so much as you, but then I was born under this desert moon."

"I don't think it's entirely the moon."

He reached over and laid his hand on the back of her neck, under her hair, gently caressing her nape. She found his touch both soothing and erotic, but couldn't tell him so. Maybe if she didn't confess to him how he made her feel, the magic would last longer.

"How did we get into this discussion, anyway?" she asked.

He chuckled. "Gert doesn't know what she missed."

Picturing the psychiatrist in the back of the extended cab, listening, she smiled. Somehow Shane had managed to reduce her brother's offense to a private joke, just between the two of them.

She felt closer to Shane than to anyone. Her smile faded. Rather than a comfort, it was a warning signal.

Chapter Ten

Since Sage had left a note on the kitchen table reminding them the Girl Scout outing at Pyramid Lake was the next day, Laura went to bed knowing they wouldn't be riding after mustangs in the morning.

Despite a lingering good-night kiss from Shane that weakened her knees, if not her resolve, she took herself off to bed in her own room, not waking until well after the sun was up.

While she dressed, she searched her mind for any lingering scraps of scout lore she might have retained from her childhood, coming up with nothing more helpful than right over left and under, then left over right and under—how to tie a square knot. Which didn't seem to have much to do with a cookout.

To tell the truth she was just as glad not to be alone with Shane today. Togetherness had gotten her to a place so unfamiliar she wasn't sure she wanted to be there.

When Laura got to the kitchen she found everyone had already eaten, but there was hot coffee left. Sipping it from a mug, she made herself toast and was spreading peanut butter on it when Sage came in.

"That looks good, maybe I'll make myself some," Sage told her.

"I overslept. Where is everyone?"

"Shane's carving some more animals for the Outpost, and Grandfather went shopping in Reno. I usually go with him but not today on account of the cookout. Shane told me not to wake you up 'cause you were worn out. Are you still?"

Laura smiled. "Not enough to need a retread."

"Good, 'cause I told everybody in my scout troop you were coming today. We got to leave in two hours. I'm going to feed Star just before we go, and Grandfather'll be back in time for his next feeding. Star knows me, and he likes me better'n anybody, but he doesn't mind Grandfather."

After they finished the toast and peanut butter, Laura went out with Sage to take a look at the baby mustang. "He's really growing fast," she told the girl.

"I can't ride him till he's at least two years old, though. That's a really, really long way off. I'll practically be a teenager. I don't plan to be obnoxious, though, like some I know.''

''I should hope not. Being obnoxious takes way too much effort.''

Sage grinned at her. ''Shane wouldn't let me anyway and, besides, I'd never be obnoxious to you.''

Putting an arm over the girl's shoulders, Laura said, ''Where is Shane's workshop?''

''It's next to the other end of the barn. Want to go see?''

''I wouldn't want to disturb him.''

''Oh, you won't do that when he's carving 'cause he doesn't even know you're there. It's kind of like he goes into a trance. Grandfather says that's 'cause he's listening to the wood talk to him, telling him what animal's in there and how it wants to look.''

Sage obviously accepted this as a perfectly normal explanation and, thinking over what Shane had told her, Laura decided it was as good as anything she could come up with.

She followed Sage from the barn and around to a small building with an open door. ''I'll just peek in,'' she told the girl.

Shane was sitting on a stool running his hands over a fair-sized piece of light-colored wood, so intent on what he was doing that he didn't look up when Laura stuck her head through the open door. He was frowning slightly, his head tilted as though he were, indeed, listening.

She stood for several moments, as engrossed in watching him as he was with the wood. She'd never paid much attention to men's hands before. His were square with long fingers, powerful hands that were also artist's hands. As well as the hands of a lover....

Feeling heat rise in her, she turned abruptly and walked away. Is this what happened once you made love with a man? That every time you saw him, arousing thoughts popped into your head?

"Hey, wait," Sage called from behind her. "You're going too fast."

Which had the ring of truth, as applied to her recent behavior as well as her present pace.

Later, helping Shane and Sage unload at the lakeside cookout site, Laura kept glancing at the weird, grayish-white encrusted formations sticking out of the water around the lake.

"What are those?" she asked finally, pointing.

"They're tufa formations, hardened mineral," Shane said. "The pyramid-shaped one over there is what the lake was named after, though not by us."

"By explorer John Frémont in 1844," Sage added triumphantly. "That was one of the questions on our history exam, and I got it right."

The large blue-green lake had none of the beauty of Lake Tahoe, up in the mountains, but Laura decided it had a certain stark grandeur, set as it was among all but barren hills. "Do the cutthroat trout you mentioned to Nathan live in the lake?" she asked.

"We're trying to reestablish them."

A van pulled up, discharging five girls who swooped down on them. Sage followed them to the edge of the water, where they all took off their shoes to wade.

More cars dropped off girls until there were ten cavorting barefoot in the lake shallows, shrieking, and laughing.

"Listen up!" Shane shouted. "It's time to get the fires started." When they'd gathered around him, he said, "There'll be two fires, so you'll split into teams of five each. I'll do the choosing."

In nothing flat he had five girls gathered around him, the other five around Laura. "If we were in the mountains we'd have lots of wood for fires," he said. "The desert's not so generous. We could find fuel to burn if we had to, but it's important not to disturb the plants around here, so we're going to cheat and use charcoal."

"On the Plains, they used to use dried buffalo chips," one of the girls said.

"You know what those chips really are," another commented and both groups burst into giggles.

Soon Shane had teams arranging the rocks around each of the two mounds of charcoal. He then demonstrated the safest way to start a charcoal fire at one of them.

"Now," he said, "we'll pretend Laura doesn't know anything about this. My team gets to tell her how to start her fire, step by step, and her team gets to correct their mistakes."

Once the charcoal was glowing, the girls laid the

grill over the fire, being careful to balance it on the rock containment. Then each scout wrapped her ear of corn in foil and seasoned her meat patty.

Laura cooked her patty right along with the girls, layering the meat between two slabs of Indian bread when it was done. The corn on the cob wrapped in aluminum foil took a bit longer.

While all this was going on, Shane discussed how food would have been cooked in the old days, asking questions of each of the girls. Laura was amazed by his patience with them.

"Man, this is way easier," one of them said.

"Next time, we'll try it the old way," Shane said. "Then you can tell me whether easier tastes better or not."

Toasted marshmallows came last, their sweet, hot stickiness reminding Laura of her girlhood camp days. "We used to sit around a campfire and tell stories after we ate," she reminisced.

"We got two fires," Sage said. "So how about if we get two sets of stories? Shane's team can tell Paiute stories and Laura's team other stories."

"Okay, if we take turns going back and forth," a girl said. "Who goes first?"

Remembering a children's counting game, Laura volunteered to do the one potato, two potato rhyme. The scout she ended with, Maria, got to be the first to tell a story.

"Well, this was a long time ago," Maria said, "when the animals could talk like people. Everyone but Black Spider was afraid of Scorpion because of his sting. She wasn't 'cause she had a poison bite, so they became friends. Then everybody got twice as scared.''

The story went on to tell how Coyote tricked the two into becoming enemies. ''And they still are right now today,'' Maria finished. ''Lucky for us.''

As the storytelling went on, Laura was struck by the difference in Paiute tales and the ones her team was telling, which sometimes seemed to be rehashed TV episodes. Then it came time for Shane to tell one.

''When the animals could talk,'' he said, ''one day Coyote decided to catch Cotton-Tail and eat her for supper, even though Wolf had warned them not to eat one another. Since he knew she was faster than he was, Coyote had to be clever. Jack-Rabbit learned of the ruses Coyote planned, and he tried to warn Cotton-Tail, but she was so sure she could outsmart Coyote that she wouldn't listen.''

The story told of several narrow escapes before Coyote finally trapped Cotton-Tail and ate her for supper. ''That made Wolf so mad about being disobeyed that he took away the animals' ability to speak and made people to replace them,'' he finished. ''Whose fault was this?''

''Coyote's,'' a chorus of voices answered.

''Yes,'' he agreed, ''but Cotton-Tail was partly to blame, too, because she refused to listen to someone who wanted to help.''

Laura had the feeling his story was meant for her, but she didn't have a chance to think about it because her turn came next. What on earth kind of story could she come up with that would top his? Obviously no condensed fairy tale would do it. She decided to tell Tim's story, softened some and changed a little. She started by saying, "Once there was a stuffed green frog named Frederick Ferdinand."

Though she'd meant to tell how Tim acquired the frog, instead she found herself saying, "Freddie lived with a little girl who loved him the most of all her toys, but after awhile she got scared that something bad would happen because she liked Freddie too much and so she gave him away. Even though she didn't want to, she knew it was the only way to save herself."

Laura stopped, realizing she'd gotten badly off track. Rattled at what she'd said, it took considerable effort for her to force the story back into the pattern she'd intended, telling how Freddie the Frog finally came to be a little boy's best friend. "Because, you see," she ended, "even though bad things had happened to him in the past, Tim wasn't afraid to keep what he loved."

There was a silence when she finished, broken by Sage saying, "That's a really sad story."

"Why? Tim got to keep the frog," Laura protested.

"But the little girl gave him away so she didn't have anything," Sage said. "That's sad."

There was a moment's silence until one of the girls said, "Let's sing."

Everybody, including Laura, thought that was a great idea. Sage's words still echoed disturbingly in her mind and she needed a distraction.

She was pleased to find the girls knew many of the old camp songs she recalled, and she sang along with them.

"Time to make sure the fires are completely out," Shane said, when there was a pause. "Each team is responsible for its own fire. Then each team gets to check how good a job the other did."

With the lake close at hand, water took care of any remaining hot coals. As they were finishing the task, parents began arriving to pick up their daughters.

"I liked being on your team," one of the girls told Laura and was echoed by others.

"I hope you come again," Maria said. "Shane doesn't know the words to the songs as good as you do."

"I hope I can," Laura told her truthfully. Though she knew she couldn't make any promises, she'd really enjoyed the afternoon with the scouts. And Shane. It had almost seemed like they were a family, the two of them and Sage, parents taking the time and effort to help out with the scout troop their daughter was in.

Of course they weren't a family at all, even if it had felt that way. For some reason the thought depressed her.

Back at the house, Sage dashed to the barn to

check on Star, leaving Shane and Laura to unload the truck.

"I'll take you as a partner any day," he said. "Especially since you know more of the words to the songs than I do."

She smiled at him. "I suspect you just like someone who follows your lead without complaining."

"Who doesn't?"

He had a point, she admitted. "I had a good time."

Shane grinned. "You made the day for Sage—and, I suspect, most of the other scouts." He didn't add that, for him, her being there had added a lot of points to his own evaluation of the day.

As they walked toward the house, she said, "I looked in your workroom earlier. Did you discover the secret inside that piece of wood you were examining?"

"I'm not sure," he said slowly, unused to talking about what he hadn't begun to work on yet.

"Maybe it's too early for me to be asking," she said, as though reading his thoughts. "Don't tell me until you're ready."

He nodded. Her sensitivity about his work made him rethink what he'd intended to bring up this evening—the beginning of her story about giving away her frog. Instead of probing, he ought to grant her the same option of not telling him until she was ready.

Once inside, since neither of them was hungry, Laura proposed making popcorn. After it was done, leaving some in the kitchen for Grandfather and Sage, they took the bowl, along with iced tea, to the front porch.

"Will we be riding out tomorrow?" she asked, after an interval of comfortable silence.

He shook his head. "I need to get ahead on my carving. I've got a couple pieces already started—a day of work'll finish them."

"I think I'll take Sage into Reno and do some shopping, then. She's outgrown most of her summer clothes."

"How much will you need?"

"My treat. I want to do this for her. Please let me."

Shane wiped his hands on a paper napkin, finished the last of his tea, stood up and offered her his hand. "Care to take a walk?"

She put her hand in his, and he pulled her to her feet, not letting go as they strolled along side by side. Her hand felt deceptively fragile in his. He'd learned she wasn't, but the smallness of her hand compared to his prompted a surge of protectiveness.

"Nevada nights are fantastic," she murmured. "So many more stars to be seen."

"And the moon." He nodded toward its rim, just visible as it edged over a hill.

"You and that moon. I think it gives you ideas."

"Don't blame it on the moon. The ideas are already there, waiting. Have to admit moonlight makes them more urgent, though."

Skirting the row of cottonwoods planted near the

house, he led her along a path that led toward the vegetable garden, and stopped by the fence.

Laura drew in a deep breath. "What's that sweet fragrance?"

"Honeysuckle. I planted the vine here so it had the fence to climb. Our mother loved the smell of honeysuckle—she grew this in a pot from a shoot someone gave her."

"What was she like?"

"I like to remember her as she was before she married Sage's father. He killed her spirit. I'll never forgive him."

With an effort, Shane banished the darkness that came over him when he thought of his stepfather. After their mother had died, he was all set to find and kill the bastard. Grandfather had kept him from going after Jennings by forcing him to remember he was the only person Sage had to count on.

"Thank you," he told Laura.

"You're welcome, but I don't know what I did to be thanked for."

"You married me and kept Sage safe." He wasn't going to get into the rest of it. His need for her had escalated from chronic to acute since that night they had camped under the moon. But he wasn't at all sure she wanted to know that. Or that he wanted to tell her.

She didn't reply and was silent so long that he put his knuckles gently under her chin and turned her face up so he could see her expression in the moonlight. Which was a mistake, because then he couldn't resist kissing her.

Her immediate response arrowed through him. He deepened the kiss, drawing her into his arms. The honeysuckle scent surrounding them made him think, for a fleeting moment, that his mother would have liked and approved of Laura.

Then, aroused by the feel of her softness against him, he forgot everything else. She tasted so sweet. And he needed more, needed the two of them naked, flesh to flesh while they made love to each other.

What he really wanted was for her to share his bed, not only tonight, but every night. When he reached out in the night he wanted Laura, warm and responsive, next to him.

His lips left hers, traveling up until he could whisper in her ear, "Tell me what you want."

"I want you to hold me forever," she murmured. "Nothing bad can happen when you hold me."

He raised his head, reminded of the story at the cookout. "Don't worry. I won't let you give me away."

A moment later he cursed himself for saying it, because she stiffened in his embrace and pulled free.

"We shouldn't be doing this," she said.

"Why not? It's perfectly legal."

"That's not the point and you know it."

"Do I?"

She turned away from him and sat on the bench. "You know why we married."

He eased down beside her but didn't touch her. "What happened while we were camping rendered the agreement you insisted on null and void."

"Our marriage still isn't a permanent arrangement. I won't be around forever."

He took her hand and began playing with her fingers. "Is that any reason we can't make love while you're here?"

"I don't think it's wise."

"What's wisdom got to do with it?"

"Now you're teasing me instead of being serious."

He brought her hand to his mouth and began kissing her fingers and heard her catch her breath. "I very much want to make love to you, and I'd lay odds you want me to."

"That's not the point."

He began touching his tongue to the webs between her fingers in lieu of an answer.

She sighed. "Oh, Shane, you make it so difficult for me to be sensible."

"If you were naked in my bed," he murmured, "I could taste you all over."

Listening to his provocative words, Laura felt as though her insides had melted. *In his bed.* Much as she longed to be there, she was afraid. Once she agreed to that, what else would she be agreeing to as well?

And then what would happen? Happy ever after? No, not her.

"I think it's dangerous to get any more attached to each other than we are already," she said firmly, withdrawing her hand and rising from the bench.

He rose, too, putting his hands on her shoulders.

"You're wrong. I don't know what in the past your fear comes from, but it has nothing to do with you and me. I'll never hurt you."

"It isn't you!" she cried. "You don't understand!" Twisting away, she fled from him up the path and into the house and the security of her own bedroom where she cried herself to sleep.

Chapter Eleven

Sage, thrilled with the idea of shopping in Reno with Laura, chattered all the way into town. Which suited Laura, since she hadn't slept well and was feeling unaccountably depressed.

"Jessica's gone back to work," Sage said. "They're going to send her to London next. Donna thinks that's way cool."

"Don't you?" Laura asked.

"Maybe I'll want to go places like that when I'm as old as Jessica."

Laura glanced at Sage. "But not now?"

Sage shook her head. "Star needs me, and I want to watch him grow up and get old enough so I can ride him. Grandfather said I'll be able to train him myself 'cause he'll trust me. That's important with

horses—they got to learn to trust you." Sage
paused. "Shane said it's the same way with people.
You got to learn to trust somebody before you can
be friends. And she has to trust you, too."

"I'd agree with that."

"Yeah, but then Grandfather said something I
didn't understand. He wasn't really talking to me,
he was talking to Shane. Anyway, he told Shane
'friends' wasn't enough. And Shane said he knew
that. Grandfather started to say something else, but
then he looked at me in his get lost kind of way, so
I did."

"I wouldn't worry about it."

Sage shrugged. "I'm not."

But maybe I should, Laura thought, strongly suspecting Grandfather had meant her. Was he up to
something? If so, she couldn't imagine what it
would be.

"Grandfather knows lots of things no one else
does," Sage went on. "That's 'cause he's a medicine man. Once in a while he even dreams. You
know most dreams don't mean anything but sometimes one does. He can tell the difference between
a true dream and just a plain ordinary one."

"I certainly wouldn't be able to."

"Me neither. You know, just before you came I
overheard Grandfather tell Shane he'd dreamed
about a palomino horse standing on our porch. He
thought that might be a true dream only he couldn't
understand it. But after you got here, I began wondering if the dream meant you were coming. I mean

we don't have one single palomino on the res so couldn't it've meant a stranger was going to arrive— a blond one?''

"I may be blond, but I'm no mystic, Sage. I'd say we should leave the dreams to Grandfather.'' Changing the subject, Laura added, "I hope you know a good place to have lunch in Reno because I'm not all that familiar with the city.''

"You mean I get to pick where we eat? Grandfather never lets me.''

"Since he's not with us, the choice is yours.''

"It's more fun to be with you.''

"That's because we're both females. Men don't always understand.''

"Yeah, but it's 'cause you're Laura, too.''

Laura felt a pang of remorse. Was she letting Sage get too fond of her?

In his workshop, Shane had made the first few cuts into the wood hiding the coyote he'd found inside it—the old Trickster himself—when Grandfather eased onto the stool next to his. Shane went on with what he was doing, undisturbed.

After a time, Grandfather said, "Long, long ago, a maiden came among the people carrying a burden basket. An old couple welcomed her into their lodge, fed and sheltered her, and named her Lonely-She-Walks. Though the maiden helped the old woman with tanning hides, gathering pine nuts, and making baskets, never once did she let anyone see what was in her own basket, the one she carried everywhere she went.

"Now it happens, Lonely-She-Walks was pretty enough to attract young men. Though she was pleasant to them all, she favored none, not until the man named Hunter came back to his people after a trading trip to the west. She smiled on Hunter, and he was smitten."

Grandfather paused and Shane, hacking away at the wood, nodded to show he was listening.

"Gray Owl, the old medicine man," Grandfather continued, "who'd been watching the maiden since her arrival in the village, had noticed that every few days just before dusk she walked up a hill and down the other side until she was out of sight.

"One evening he took it upon himself to follow, and hidden, watched as, weeping, she took off the lid of the basket. Though nothing could be seen coming out, Lonely-She-Walks fell back as though something had pushed her over. When she finally sat up again, she was pale. She replaced the lid on the basket and rose just as the first star appeared.

"What he'd watched struck Gray Owl as ominous. When she returned to the village, he came out of hiding and crept back unobserved. When it became clear to him that Hunter meant to marry the maiden, he took the man aside and warned him he must not marry this woman until she revealed the contents of her basket to him or calamity would result.

"Hunter listened to the extent of asking Lonely-

She-Walks what was inside her burden basket. But when she refused to tell him, saying if he truly loved her, he wouldn't need to know, he ignored the medicine man's advice and married her anyway. Gray Owl's words, though, had entered the man's heart, darkening it, and he determined to find out on his own what was inside the burden basket she guarded so carefully.

"Waiting until she slept, Hunter crept from the blankets to where the basket rested within reach of her hand. Lifting it, he bore the basket to the door of the lodge where the moonlight shone in. Raising the cover of rushes, he peered inside. To his surprise he saw nothing—the basket was empty. His heart unsettled, he returned the basket to its place. In the morning, he consulted Gray Owl.

"'Inside are her ghosts,' the old man told him. 'Only Lonely-She-Walks can see them. Sooner or later they will suck her life away and she will die.'

"Hunter wanted to dispose of the basket, but Gray Owl warned him that the ghosts would remain. Not unless he could persuade Lonely-She-Walks that they were destroyed would she ever be free. When Hunter told his wife he knew she carried ghosts, she turned her face from him and would not speak.

"That night, when she thought he slept, she tried to leave with her basket, but Hunter was watching. Remembering what Gray Owl had told him, he grabbed the basket, flung off the top and one by one pulled the ghosts he couldn't see or feel from the basket and tossed them onto the coals of the fire, saying, 'I have destroyed them.'"

Shane waited, but Grandfather said no more.

"I've never heard that story before," he told the old man. "I presume they lived happily ever after?"

"No man and no woman are happy one hundred percent of the time. Life sees to that. The story is a parable, as you must know if you have any brains in that thick head of yours." Grandfather rose from the stool and left the workshop.

Shane turned the wood in his hands, seeing how the coyote would look, while he thought about the story. He understood perfectly what Grandfather had told him. But it was one clever man who could destroy ghosts he couldn't see or feel because they belonged to someone else.

He knew Laura would leave him if he couldn't find a way to get her to talk about what it was in her past that troubled her, making her afraid to love. No matter how he'd tried to convince himself he wanted her to stay with him out of pure lust, in his heart he understood lust was only a small part of it.

Damned if he hadn't gone and fallen in love with the woman. She belonged here with him, no matter how she tried to deny it. The denial, he felt, didn't come from the Laura he held in his arms, the person who responded so sweetly to him. No, it came from another Laura, one terrified of the past, one who denied love because she feared what might happen.

He whittled away at the wood as he tried to figure what to do and eventually Coyote's laughing face stared out at him. "Trickster," he muttered. "You don't always win."

No, not always, but too often.

In the late afternoon, Laura and Sage sang along with the radio all the way back from Reno. The girl's obvious pleasure in the outing had lightened Laura's mood, and they'd had fun together.

As they pulled into the drive, Sage said, "Shane's truck is gone, I wonder where he went. Are you two going after the mustangs tomorrow?"

"He said something about delivering his carvings to the Outpost before noon tomorrow," Laura told her. "It'll probably be the day after before we ride out again."

"Good. Maria's having a dessert potluck party next week, and I'm supposed to bring cookies. Maybe you can help me learn to make a new kind. I want to surprise everybody."

"Glad to help. What kind of cookies do you have in mind?"

They were still discussing cookies when they came into the house laden with shopping loot. Shane was nowhere in sight. Grandfather, though, was drinking iced tea in the kitchen.

"That little colt of yours sure missed you," he told Sage.

She immediately dumped her packages onto the kitchen table and dashed off. Laura picked them up and brought them into Sage's room, leaving the packages on her bed. She left her own in her room.

When she returned to the kitchen she found Grandfather had poured her a glass of iced tea so she sat down at the table.

"No sugar," he said.

She smiled.

"When you first came here you reminded me of a woman in one of our stories," he told her. "Now, I'm not so sure. Still, you could go back to being like that woman."

Laura raised her eyebrows. "I'm not sure I understand."

"Her name was Lonely-She-Walks."

It took her several moments to decipher what he was getting at. "I'm not lonely," she protested.

"Why should you be? You have Sage and me right here and you have Shane. But if you leave us, then who do you have?"

My brother, she wanted to say. My parents. The words didn't come. The old man spoke the truth. Without Shane, what did she have? Sage and Grandfather were the bonus that came with him, but Shane was the heart.

"When we married—" she began.

Grandfather shook his head. "You both have come far past any wedding agreements. If you leave, you'll break Sage's heart. Still, she's young and will in time recover. Shane won't."

"He doesn't—"

"You don't understand him. I do. He is not a man who gives his heart easily."

Laura swallowed. "But I have commitments. I

have to finish my work with the wild mustangs. In fact, I'm planning to go to Montana when I leave here. I—'' she broke off, seeing Sage's stricken face. Unknown to her, the girl had reentered the kitchen.

''You're going to Montana?'' Sage asked.

Laura nodded, planning to explain, but before she could, Sage whirled and ran from the room.

Laura got to her feet as Grandfather rose. ''She'll be with the colt,'' he said. ''I'll see to her.''

Unable to decide what to do, since he'd taken away the initiative, Laura automatically took the two glasses to the sink and rinsed them out. She hadn't meant to hurt Sage—it was the last thing in the world she wanted to do.

Grandfather's words about breaking Sage's heart replayed themselves in her mind, making her feel terrible. And what had he meant about Shane?

As if thinking about him had evoked him, Shane came into the kitchen carrying a large pizza box, which he set on the table. ''I figured neither you nor Sage would feel like cooking,'' he said. ''Grandfather said he didn't either and that he had a taste for pizza, so here it is.''

''That's good,'' she managed to say.

''I detect a marked lack of enthusiasm. What's the matter?''

''Oh, Shane, I hurt Sage. I didn't mean to, but—''

''Hurt her? You mean you had an accident?''

''No, no, nothing like that. I was telling Grandfather I intended to go to Montana when I finished here. She overheard me and dashed out before I could explain.''

''I'm here. You can explain to me.''

Laura swallowed, staring at his suddenly expressionless face. His eyes looked as hard as obsidian.

''Well, you know I'm working with this federal grant, and—''

His hand slashed the air, dismissing the grant.

''I have to go where the mustangs are,'' she said.

''What about the other Nevada herds?''

''Yes, I know, but it seemed like a good idea to go to Montana first.''

''Running away.''

''I'm not!'' She glowered at him.

''The hell you aren't. You're running scared, don't try to deny it.''

''But you know I won't always be here. I thought I should try to get Sage used to the idea I'd be coming and going.''

''How did you plan to get her used to the idea that one of those 'going' times you won't be coming back?''

''I'm fond of Sage,'' she cried. ''I don't want to hurt her.''

''Or me?''

Taken aback, she stammered, ''But you—you're not a child.''

''What's that have to do with it?''

''You're not being reasonable. It's not as though we promised to stay together forever.''

"Actually we did. Didn't you hear the JP's words when he married us?"

She'd been in a daze at the time, but she knew what the words in a marriage ceremony usually were. *Till death do us part.*

"But we both agreed we weren't really married."

He shook his head. "I agreed not to expect you in my bed until you came there voluntarily. Otherwise, to me it was and is a marriage."

Laura stared at him.

"I knew you had this grant work to finish," he said, "but I expected you meant to follow a logical sequence and check out the Nevada herds first."

"I'm going to come back to do that," she insisted.

"Are you?"

Laura drew herself up. "Of course. I promised you I'd be around long enough to ensure that you'd have no problem with keeping Sage's custody permanent."

"Dropping by every other weekend to say hi?"

"What's the matter with you anyway?" she cried.

"The problem doesn't lie with me." He spun on his heel and left.

Later, when Grandfather and Sage came in for supper, Shane didn't appear. "Want me to call him?" Sage asked.

Grandfather shook his head. "He's in his workshop. He'll eat when he gets hungry enough. If we leave him any pizza, that is."

Though Laura tried to eat, between Sage refusing

to speak to her and her own troubled thoughts, she couldn't manage to finish even one slice of pizza. Much as she wanted to escape to her room, she felt the least she could do was clean up the kitchen. Both of them left her to it.

As she was finishing, Grandfather wandered back into the kitchen. "Maybe we need to sit on the porch and talk," he said.

"I'm rather tired—" she began.

"No you're not, you just don't want to hear any more good advice from me," he said.

That made her smile ruefully. "I'm afraid you're right."

"Come sit with me anyway. Who knows, it's possible I may find some bad advice you'd like better."

She'd never been able to resist Grandfather, so she reluctantly followed him out to the porch.

"Thinking of getting us another dog," he said, when they'd settled into chairs. "The last one died of old age about a month before you came. Part Border collie, she was, but bigger. A good dog. And smart. You can't keep a little dog out here. Coyotes get 'em. So the new one'll have to be a good-sized one, at least half-grown, to be big enough to discourage a coyote."

Laura was horrified. "You mean the coyotes kill little dogs?"

Grandfather nodded. "To a coyote anything smaller than he is becomes what nowadays they call part of the food chain. You can't blame them, that's their way. Earth nourishes every one of us in one way or another.''

''I suppose.'' Laura didn't care to dwell on what coyotes ate. ''Hunger is a basic drive, after all.''

''For us, so is love. Why can't you love, Laura?''

She should have seen it coming, but hadn't. Grandfather had ambushed her again. She chose her words with care. ''I love my brother. And my parents, naturally.''

''Yes, they're safe to love because you only see them once in awhile.''

Though she wanted to deny vehemently that there was any truth in what he'd said, Laura didn't. Actually she didn't see her parents more than once a year and her brother maybe twice.

''I said that wrong,'' Grandfather told her. ''A better question is why won't you love? Please give an old man an honest answer.''

''I don't know if I can give an answer. It's just safer not to get too fond of anyone, that's all.''

''Lonely-She-Walks,'' Grandfather said as if to himself. ''Lonely-She-Walks, with her ghosts of the past in her basket.'' He turned his head and looked at her. ''Ever see a shrink?''

The time for indignation was long past. She decided to be as blunt as he was. ''Yes.''

''Did she have any good or bad advice?''

Wondering how he'd decided the shrink had been a woman, Laura said, ''She didn't offer advice, she tried to pull that out of you because she seemed to believe her patients never took anyone's advice except their own, bad or good.''

Grandfather put his head to one side, apparently considering this. Finally he said, ''Did she help you?''

Laura nodded.

''But not enough,'' he told her. ''Tonight you will dream because everyone dreams at night. Try to remember what the dream is. Then think about it. That's all the advice I have.''

Feeling dismissed, Laura rose, said good-night and fled to her room. She tried to read, but couldn't concentrate. She couldn't sleep either. In desperation she tried some relaxation exercises she'd learned, and when at last sleep wandered her way, she nabbed it....

She was in a night camp somewhere in the desert, sitting cross-legged by the coals of a fire, their winking red eyes the only light. The scent of sage mingled with the faint smell of horse, so she knew mustangs had been here earlier.

In her lap she held a covered basket, her arms protectively curved around it. When a dark figure of a man stepped out of the darkness, she clutched the basket tighter as she watched him approach. He sat down beside her near the coals and she saw he was Shane.

''The fire is almost out,'' he said. ''There's little time. Give me the basket.''

''It's mine, not yours. You can't have it.''

In the darkness a coyote began to yip. Others answered.

"They tell you to give up the basket," he said.

"I can't."

The coyotes' cries grew louder, closer. She peered apprehensively into the night and, as she did, he jerked the basket away from her.

Before she could stop him, he pulled off the lid and upended the basket over the coals. Though nothing came out that she could see, the coals sputtered and fizzed and sparked.

He tossed the basket aside and rose. "Now it's up to you," he said, striding off into the dark. She heard the singing of the coyotes fade as though they flanked him like guards.

Then there was no sound. He'd left her alone without even the coyotes. The coals winked out one by one until only a single glowing ember remained. When that one died, she knew it would mean the time had finally run out.

She rose, looking wildly about, seeing nothing, for there was nothing to see. "No!" she screamed....

And woke up with her heart pounding. Fighting free of the shards of the dream, she muttered, "Grandfather and his damn basket."

She could trace almost every element in the dream back to something he'd said to her and so, she told herself, the dream had no underlying meaning. But she had to admit it certainly wasn't something she was likely to forget in a hurry.

Then she couldn't go back to sleep. Since it was

still dark, there was little point in getting up. She lay there wondering if Shane was asleep in his room down the hall. How easy it would be to ease from her bed and go to his. How surprised he'd be to find her there. Not too surprised to make love to her, though, not Shane. She wondered if he slept in the nude. Imagining it made the treacherous warmth pool deep inside her, urging her to go to him.

Only Shane could relieve the ache of need.

But she would never go to his bed, no matter how much she wanted to.

Chapter Twelve

Sage was alone in the kitchen when Laura wandered out for breakfast. She smiled, hoping the girl would talk to her, but she didn't expect Sage's outburst.

"Am I ever glad you're up!" Sage said, obviously upset. "After Grandfather went to the Outpost with Shane, I got a funny phone call."

Thinking she meant obscene, Laura worded her question carefully. "Was it a man?"

Sage nodded.

"Did he say things that you didn't want to hear?"

"No, it's just that he asked for Shane and when I said Shane wasn't here he asked for Howell and I sort of forgot that was Grandfather's name 'cause no one ever calls him that. But finally I remembered and told him Grandfather wasn't here either. So then he asked if I was Elizabeth.'' Sage paused and stared at Laura, her eyes wide and frightened.

"Elizabeth?"

"Yeah, that was the name on my birth certificate, Elizabeth Sage Jennings. Shane helped our mom to get my last name changed to Bearclaw before she died. I guess I'm still Elizabeth, but nobody ever calls me that.''

A possibility occurred to Laura. "Could the man have been your father?''

Sage jumped up from her chair and ran to Laura, who put an arm around her.

"Don't be frightened, I'm here,'' Laura told her.

"But what if it *is* him?''

"What did you tell the man?'' Laura asked.

"I said my name was Sage and I hung up. The phone rang again, but I let the answering machine take it. I'm scared to go listen and see if he left a message.''

"I think we'd better find out.'' Trailed by Sage, Laura headed for Shane's bedroom, where she'd been told the answering machine was.

She'd never set foot in his room before, but intent on listening to a possible message, she didn't take time to look around. She crossed to the machine. The red light was blinking so she pushed the button.

"Connie and I are coming by to see you, Sage,'' a man's voice said. "We have a birthday present for you.''

"My birthday's not till next month,'' Sage muttered, her gaze fixed on the answering machine. "Doesn't he even know that?"

"So it is your father," Laura said.

"Yeah. He said in the letter he wrote to Shane that his new wife was named Connie."

"What's his name?" Laura asked, figuring she should know before the couple showed up.

"Bill." Sage reached for Laura's hand. "What're we going to do?"

Holding the girl's hand firmly in hers, Laura led her from the bedroom, glancing down as she did at what she was wearing. Khaki shorts and a yellow T-shirt. That ought to do for Mr. and Mrs. Jennings.

"We're going to make a pitcher of iced tea, invite them in when they come and offer them some tea," she told Sage.

"But I don't want them here," Sage wailed.

"Nothing bad will happen. The judge has granted Shane custody of you."

Sage's fingers tightened on hers. "Yeah, but how do I know my father won't ab-abduct me like those kids I see on milk cartons?"

"I doubt if he has that in mind." Laura tried her best to sound reassuring when the truth was she didn't have a clue what this unknown man was like.

"He used to hurt my mom." Sage spoke in a whisper.

"I am *not* going to let anything bad happen to you," Laura said, beginning to be affected by the girl's apprehension.

"I wish Shane was here," Sage wailed and burst into tears.

Laura couldn't help but wish the same thing as she held the sobbing girl close. She tried to tell herself that Bill Jennings might once have been a belligerent drunk, but supposedly he'd stopped drinking and turned his life around. Besides, he had his wife with him.

When Sage had progressed to the sniffling stage, blowing her nose and wiping her eyes, Laura said, "I've decided we should believe that your father is coming to see you for exactly the reason he said he was—bringing you a present."

"Maybe." Sage didn't sound convinced. "But why did he wait till Shane and Grandfather were gone?"

"It's possible he called and asked for them because he wanted to tell one or the other of them ahead of time that he was coming here—not to find out if they were away."

Sage blinked at her, looking so woebegone that Laura felt her heart twist. She hugged the girl. "It'll be all right," she said, hoping she spoke the truth. "Now let's go make that iced tea. And I'm in real and immediate need of a cup of coffee."

"I got to go feed Star first," Sage said.

"Okay, I'll hold down the fort."

After Sage went out, Laura reflected that she felt she was doing just that—holding down the fort against hostiles. Except in the old days, hadn't the Indians been the hostiles? A little role reversal, here.

Revived by the coffee, Laura took a quick walk through the house to make sure it didn't look too untidy, picking up things here and there and putting them where they belonged. By the time she was through, Sage was back in the kitchen making the tea with a resigned look on her face. Sullen was better than scared, though.

"We ought to try to be polite," she reminded the girl.

Sage's glance told her not to expect any such thing.

Because she wasn't at ease, it seemed to Laura that the Jennings took forever to arrive. When they finally heard a car engine, Sage ran to the window to watch them turn into the drive.

"They've got a van," she announced. "A black one. Vans come in handy if you're thinking of abducting people, don't you think?"

"What I think is that your imagination is running wild. You were such a gracious hostess when I first came here. Make an effort to be like that for them."

"Yeah, but I liked you."

"I was a stranger," Laura reminded her. "You didn't even know me."

"I sort of did. Grandfather said you might be the palomino from his dream and that would be good luck for us. When I saw your blond hair I knew he was right."

Footsteps on the porch made them both come to uneasy attention. Then came the knock.

Laura crossed to the door and opened it. A somewhat overweight middle-aged man who was beginning to lose his graying hair stood beside a pleasant-faced younger woman who was obviously pregnant.

"Mr. and Mrs. Jennings?" she said. "I'm Laura—" She started to say Walker, decided that might be confusing, and substituted, "Bearclaw. Won't you come in?"

She ushered them into the living room with Sage doing her best to hide behind her.

"Elizabeth," Bill Jennings said, holding out his hand. "Don't you know me?"

The girl retreated from him. "My name is Sage," she said, "not Elizabeth. And I know you must be my father even if I don't recognize you."

Not the most gracious of responses, but at least Sage was talking to him.

"This is my wife, Connie," Bill said. "Your new stepmother."

Sage frowned at the woman.

"Please sit down," Laura said hastily, not sure the girl wasn't going to blurt out something unpleasant. "Sage has made iced tea for you." She glanced at the girl. "Why don't you bring it in?"

Watching Sage hurry from the room, Laura hoped she'd return and not go hide somewhere.

"I'm afraid your daughter is a bit overwhelmed at your sudden appearance," she told the couple.

Bill sighed. "I've been a rotten father. Rotten altogether, some might say. If I hadn't met Connie I don't know what would've become of me and that's the truth." He smiled at his wife.

Laura decided she may as well state the obvious. "It will take Sage some time to get used to you." Fixing her attention on Connie she said, "I couldn't help but notice you're expecting."

Connie's smile was shy. "It's my first. I'm due in October."

"A Halloween baby," Bill said. "Connie here said we ought to get to know Eliz—Sage. The new baby will be her half brother, after all. Like Shane is."

Laura didn't think Sage would take kindly to the comparison between Shane and the baby-to-come. "So you already know it's a boy," she said.

Connie nodded. "I didn't care, I just want a healthy baby. Bill's kind of pleased, though."

"You bet. Sage and little Joe'll have something else in common, too. Connie here is a quarter Miwok."

Laura remembered Grandfather telling her about Connie's Miwok heritage.

"My mother's people still live in central California," Connie said. "I thought maybe Sage would feel more at home with us if she knew that about me, so that's why Bill told you right away."

Sage came into the room with the tray, which she placed on the coffee table in front of the couch where the Jennings sat.

"I didn't know about sugar," she said, "so I didn't put any in the tea."

"Thank you, honey," Connie said. "I'm not supposed to have any while I'm pregnant."

Sage eyed Connie's abdomen warily.

"It's a boy," Bill told her. "We're going to name him Joel William."

Watching Sage, Laura could almost see what was running through the girl's mind—that she and the baby would be related.

"I'd like some sweetener, if you don't mind," Bill added.

Without a word, Sage turned on her heel and headed for the kitchen.

"The message you left was that you were bringing Sage a present," Laura said. "She mentioned that her birthday is next month."

Bill shook his head. "Told you I've been the world's worst father. I knew it was in the summer sometime and took a chance it was this month. Well, she'll get it early, that's all."

Though not exactly warming to him, Laura found herself feeling a bit sorry for Bill. He'd missed so many years of his daughter's childhood and was now going to have a really hard time winning her trust. Connie she rather liked. Laura couldn't feel these were bad people.

"I left your present in the van," Bill told Sage when she returned with several packets of sweetener and a spoon. "Remind me to give it to you before we leave. Sorry I was wrong about your birthday."

"That's okay," she mumbled.

"I thought maybe you might send me a school picture sometime," Bill said to her. "I'll leave my card here so you'll have my address." Removing one from his wallet, he laid it on the coffee table.

Sage nodded, not looking at him.

"I'm an electrician," he said. "That's my company name on the card."

Connie smiled at him. "What with the building boom, he's really busy these days."

Bill glanced at his watch. "That reminds me— we've got to get going. Came over the mountain for a builders' convention in Reno, and we were so close I didn't want to go back home without seeing you, Sage."

She looked him square in the face for the first time, but said nothing.

"Want to come out with us and get your present?" he asked, rising from the couch.

Sage glanced at Laura. Knowing the girl wouldn't budge unless she went, too, Laura got up and took Sage's hand.

A few minutes later, all four of them were standing by the black van when Shane's pickup roared into the drive. He cut the motor, leaped out and strode over to them.

"Just what the hell do you think you're doing here, Jennings?" he demanded.

Bill bristled. "I came to see my daughter."

"We have a present for her," Connie put in, obviously trying to do what she could to save the situation.

Outside of shooting her one quick glance, Shane

ignored her. "I don't want you on my property," he told Bill. "Not now, not ever."

The two men glared at each other.

Laura knew why Shane was overreacting, but she wished he could control himself long enough so explanations could be made.

Grandfather, who'd gotten out of the truck in less of a hurry than Shane, ambled over. "Hear you quit drinking," he said to Bill. "Past time." He turned to Sage, "Take the present your father brought, thank him, and go in the house. Now."

Hastily Connie reached into the van and brought out a colorfully wrapped box, handing it to Sage.

Holding the box, Sage mumbled, "Thank you both," and all but ran toward the house.

Grandfather stepped between the two men. "Best thing you can do right now is hop in the van and hit the road," he told Bill. "Best thing you can do," he said to Shane, "is leave well enough alone."

He turned to Connie and helped her into the van, saying, "Tell your husband this is not a good day to talk things over."

Bill slammed himself into the other side of the van and the three of them watched him drive away, Shane muttering under his breath.

Deciding the best thing for her to do was join Sage while Shane cooled off, Laura left the two men. She found the girl in the kitchen opening the box.

"Look, it's a CD player/radio with a headset just

like the one I looked at in Reno yesterday,'' Sage said.

"So it is. A great birthday present.''

Sage tore the wrappings off a smaller packet that had been taped to the outside of the box. "Four CDs.'' She shuffled through them. "Whoa—one's by that Navajo flute player. He's way cool!''

"Connie must have picked it out," Laura said. "Your father told me Connie's grandmother is a Miwok."

Sage looked at her. "She is?" Looking back down at the CD, she said, "I guess Connie's baby'll be related to me."

Noting there was no mention of Bill, Laura realized Sage wasn't yet ready to accept her father. She didn't push it, merely saying, "Yes. Joel will be your half brother."

"Shane was real mad," Sage said.

Laura nodded. "When he calms down, I'll try to explain that your father did try to call him before he came."

"If Shane'd been here, he wouldn't've let them come."

"Probably not."

"Connie's not so bad," Sage said, without looking at Laura.

"I liked her," Laura agreed, as she began gathering up the wrapping paper and ribbon and stuffing them into the now empty box.

"I'm going to take the player and CDs to my room and try them out," Sage told her.

"Good idea. Maybe later you can let me listen to the flute player with you."

That earned her a smile before Sage left the kitchen.

Laura was setting the box and paper on the utility room floor when Grandfather came in the back door. "Where's Shane?" she asked.

"In his workshop. Best place for him."

"I'm not making a plea for Bill Jennings," she said, "but he did call before he arrived, asking for you or Shane."

"Doubt that'll make much difference to Shane."

"Did you notice Connie Jennings was pregnant?" Grandfather nodded.

"The baby will be Sage's half brother," she added.

"Doubt that'll matter to Shane either. I'm an old man, wiser than I used to be, still with things to learn. I've learned the heart isn't made to hold hate. Hate is bitter medicine, no one's the better for it. Most times you can't turn hate into love, but you can work on turning it into tolerance. If you can't even do that, you still have to let go of hate. Burn it in a fire, like Lonely-She-Walks' ghosts."

Laura frowned. "I keep hearing about Lonely-She-Walks—who was she?"

"Pour us some iced tea and I'll tell you. It's a story you need to hear."

Sitting across the kitchen table from Grandfather, sipping tea, Laura listened to the tale of the maiden with the burden basket.

She was frowning before he finished. Afterwards she sat in silence, wrapped in her own thoughts, and so preoccupied that she barely noticed when Grandfather got up and left the kitchen. Nor did she pay attention to Sage when she came in, not until the girl spoke.

"You want to come listen to the flute CD?" Sage asked. "It's really awesome."

Laura nodded and followed Sage into the bedroom where she sat on the bed. Gradually, the sound of the flute lured her into attention, making her realize how talented the man was.

She smiled, remembering how Shane had made and played a willow flute for her at their camp. He wasn't an artist like this man, but she'd never forget that night.

"You *do* like him," Sage said. "I knew you would."

Laura blinked, jerked from her reverie. "Oh, yes," she replied. "Connie made a good choice."

Sage bit her lip. "It was nice of them to give me a birthday present, but that doesn't mean I have to like him."

"No, but it does mean you have to write a thank-you note."

Scowling, Sage said, "I suppose."

"I forgot and left his card on the coffee table," Laura said, rising and opening the door, thinking she'd better get it before Shane saw it.

"That's okay. I picked it up when Grandfather

told me to go in the house 'cause I didn't want Shane to get any madder.''

"Good thinking."

"I was afraid they were going to get in a fight. It scared me. I mean, I don't like my father, but I didn't want to see Shane hit him."

"Grandfather didn't let them get that far," Laura assured her.

"You want to hear some more CDs?"

Before Laura could answer, the phone rang and Sage flew out of the room to answer it. "It's for you," she called to Laura. "Some lady."

Wondering if it might be Jade, Laura headed for the phone. "Did she give her name?" she asked Sage as the girl passed her on her way back to the bedroom.

Sage shook her head.

"This is Laura," she said into the phone.

"Connie Jennings. I'm sorry to bother you, but you're the only one I feel I can talk to. I hope you don't mind."

"No, not at all," Laura said. Suspecting she was going to be asked to play the role of peacemaker, she added, "Though I'm not sure I can help."

"I'm not sure either, but poor Bill is so disappointed, I just had to talk to you. I didn't know him when he drank, so he might have done bad things then, but he's really a good man at heart. What he wanted to talk to Shane about was having Sage visit us sometimes after the baby is born so the two of them could get to know each other."

"I'm not sure this would be a good time to discuss that with Shane."

"I realize that and so does Bill. He doesn't know I'm calling you, but I thought maybe you could try to sort of soften Shane's attitude toward Bill and maybe call me at home in Torrance when you think there might be a chance Shane would listen to Bill. The number's on the card he left."

"I really can't promise anything."

"But will you at least try? Please. It'd mean so much to Bill. He really wants to be a father to Sage as well as our baby."

"The best I think you might hope for would be supervised visits," Laura said, feeling caught in the middle.

"That would be fine. Anything."

Laura sighed. "I'll try, but..." She let her words trail off.

"Oh, thank you, thank you. I'm sure it's some consolation to Bill to have met the woman who's taking care of Sage—we both could tell you're a good person. I really appreciate you listening to me. I'll let you go now."

Laura hung up the phone feeling depressed. She understood how Shane felt and couldn't blame him. Yet she also understood how the Jennings felt and, to her mind, they had a point. How could she possibly approach Shane about the matter, though?

Certainly not today!

She could imagine Shane in his workshop hacking

away, taking his anger out on a piece of wood. What would it be—a snarling bear?

Restlessness drove her to change to riding clothes and go to the corral where she saddled Colly. Not caring to risk getting lost, she rode in the direction of the creek, landmarked for her by the line of cottonwoods.

She breathed deeply, enjoying the clean, warm air, tinged by the scent of sage cast up as the horse trotted among the bushes. An appreciation of this high desert country had crept into her blood—how she'd hate to leave here. The Paiute story Grandfather had told her lurked in the back of her mind, but she fought thinking about it. What did ghosts have to do with her?

Intent on her own thoughts, she was startled into awareness when a herd of mustangs burst from the cottonwoods and raced across her path. The bachelor herd, she realized, counting them. All five were there and, from the pace they were traveling, all in pretty good condition.

She halted the mare and watched until the mustangs vanished over a rise. Their grace and beauty touched a hidden place in her heart. Never in her life had she felt wild and free....

Sighing, she turned the mare and headed back to the house. To Sage, who needed her. To Shane, who said he needed her—but did he really?

Chapter Thirteen

As Laura was rubbing the mare down after unsaddling her, Shane came into the corral.

"I saw the bachelor herd," she told him excitedly. "Not too far from here. With luck maybe I can get a close view tomorrow."

"We."

She gave him an uneasy glance, put off by his curtness. "That's what I meant."

"You shouldn't have allowed Jennings anywhere near Sage," he told her.

Laura straightened and glared at him. "He wasn't drunk, he had his wife with him, they'd come to bring Sage a present—what harm was there in it?"

"I just don't want the man anywhere near her."

"Sage handled herself very well."

"She shouldn't have to be upset by him."

Putting her hands on her hips, she said, "The man, as you call him, is her father and she knows he is. Isn't it better for her to realize he isn't the monster she's imagined him to be?"

"He's a no-good bast—"

"Don't call him names. Whatever he was like when he drank, he's doing his best to change. Doesn't everyone deserve a second chance?"

"Not him."

Though Laura had told herself she wasn't going to be provoked into losing her temper, it slipped from her control. "And will the hate you feel for her father make you deny Sage the chance to ever meet the boy who'll be her half brother?"

Shane stared at her, speechless for a moment. He'd noticed the woman with Jennings was pregnant, but he hadn't taken the thought beyond that.

"Just how chummy did you get with them?" he snapped. "Next you'll be telling me the kid's name."

"Joel William. He's going to be a Halloween baby. I happen to believe it's important to be civil to people unless they give me reason not to be. Both the Jennings were perfectly polite. And they did call ahead and ask for you or Grandfather."

"So you took it on yourself to invite them to come to my house while I was gone."

"I did no such thing! And if I had, isn't it my house, too?"

He tried to curb his rage, aware he was getting

out of line and was getting her all riled up. "Look, just keep him away from Sage, that's all I ask."

He watched Laura take a deep breath and let it out. "He's her father. I agree Sage needs to stay here with you, she wants to and it's the best thing for her. That's why I married you, in case you've forgotten. I want you to tell me what would it hurt to let the Jennings bring the new baby here once in a while so she can get to know him. She has that right—he'll be her half brother, after all. And I think her mind would be relieved to discover her father isn't as bad as she and you both think. Maybe she'll never learn to love him, but—"

He slashed his hand through the air, all control gone. "Enough! I'll never let that man bring his kid anywhere near Sage. I'm the only damn half brother she'll ever have."

"But—"

"Not another word. A lot you know about it. What right have you to butt into what's none of your business?"

She flinched as though he'd struck her. "If that's how you feel, it's just as well I'm leaving."

A muffled sob made them both whirl. Sage stood just outside the corral. How long had she been there? How much had she heard? His anger draining away, Shane started toward her. Sage turned and ran.

Laura threw the horse cloth at him, crying, "Take care of the mare," as she dashed after Sage.

When he finished with the mare, he went in search of Grandfather, deciding it was best to let both Laura and Sage cool off. He found him standing outside the back door.

"Something's wrong with the young one," Grandfather said.

"She overheard Laura and me quarreling." Shane wiped a hand over his face. "Lost my temper."

Grandfather shook his head. "Why didn't you stay in the workroom?"

"I heard Laura come back from riding."

"Bad choice to talk to her before your mind quieted. It's never good to risk undoing what's slowly coming to be. A quiet mind is worth all the world's riches."

"I know." He gave Grandfather a rueful smile. "I haven't quite latched on to how to quiet mine."

Laura appeared in the doorway. "Is Sage out here somewhere?" she asked. "I can't find her anywhere in the house."

"Probably in the barn with Star," Shane said.

Laura frowned. "Should we let her be alone with the colt for awhile?"

Shane nodded and Laura retreated back into the house.

"I'd best let *her* be alone for awhile, too," he said to Grandfather.

"What triggered the fight?" Grandfather asked. "Your pigheadedness?"

"She has some harebrained idea that Sage should be allowed to get to know the coming baby."

"Yeah, it's always annoying to be wrong."

Shane was so sure Grandfather would agree with

him that it took him a moment to realize the old man was in tune with Laura instead.

Grandfather shrugged. "Seems to me you're carrying around your own burden basket full of past ghosts."

"But Jennings is a—"

"He was, yes. But Connie looks like a good woman and the man was stone sober, something I never before knew him to be. When we get older, some of us change for the better. He could have. Are you God to say Sage should never be allowed to know her father? Or her other half brother?"

Shane clenched his fists, whirled on his heel and stalked away from the house toward the corral. He'd saddle Cloud and ride off until he could think straight. He hadn't quarreled with Grandfather in years, and he wasn't going to start now.

When he went into the tack room inside the barn to get his saddle, he glanced over at the colt's pen. Stopping, he scanned the pen. Star was there, but he didn't see Sage. He crossed to the pen and the little horse crowded against the bars, looking for company. Sage was nowhere in sight.

Was she hiding from him? Pained by the thought, he was about to turn back to the tack room when it hit him that maybe she wasn't in the barn at all. He began a search, calling her name. After he'd poked into all the possible hiding places and didn't find her, Shane began to worry. If she wasn't in the barn, where was she? Her horse wasn't missing and her saddle was in the tack room, so she hadn't ridden off.

He checked his workroom. Not there. Nor was she in any of the other outbuildings. He strode toward the house, telling himself not to worry, she'd be there, probably shut in her room.

He entered through the back door, calling her name. Laura came from the direction of the living room. "Sage isn't in the house," she said.

"Did you check her room?"

She gave him an exasperated look. "Of course. I even searched it. Isn't she with Star?"

He shook his head.

"But where would she go?" Laura asked, alarm lacing her voice.

"I wish I knew."

Grandfather appeared. "Missing, is she?"

"Looks that way." Shane kept his voice calm with an effort.

"She wouldn't start off for Donna's house would she?" Laura asked. "That's a couple of miles away. I could get in the car and go looking for her."

Shane didn't know what to tell her.

"Sage is hiding," Grandfather said.

"I've checked all the outbuildings," Shane said.

"Then she's run off to her secret place," Grandfather told them.

"Where in hell is that?" Shane wanted to know.

Grandfather looked him in the eye. "She thinks no one knows. So I'll go alone. She won't be ready to see either of you. From what Laura told me, if

Sage overheard much of your quarrel, she has good reason not to want to have anything to do right now with her unreasonable brother. Or Laura, who's leaving her.''

Shane glanced at Laura, seeing the same pain in her eyes as he felt. ''Okay,'' he told Grandfather gruffly. ''Go find Sage.''

After the old man left the house, Shane was tempted to retreat to his workshop, but another look at Laura's strained face stopped him. He'd be leaving her alone to brood. ''I guess I sounded off pretty strong,'' he muttered, finding it hard to apologize.

''I guess you did,'' she told him.

Which left them right where they'd started.

She walked past him and into the living room. He followed, watching her sit on the couch, curling her feet up under her. Bare feet, he noticed. And she no longer wore her riding clothes—she'd changed into shorts. With an effort he kept his gaze from her legs.

Too restless to sit, he began pacing back and forth.

''Are you sure Grandfather will find Sage?'' she asked.

He tossed her a nod, then said, ''You think I was out of line?''

''Didn't I already say so?''

''Grandfather warned me not to play God.''

''A wise man.''

Shane stopped pacing to stand in front of her. ''I just don't like or trust Jennings.''

''Must you loom over me?'' she asked tartly. ''Sit

down so we can discuss this without me feeling like you're about to pounce."

Shane eased down beside her.

"I never said you had to like the man," she told him. "But I fail to see what harm could come to Sage from occasional supervised visits from the Jennings, especially if it was here on the ranch where she feels at home. At the same time, it would give you the chance to size him up and make sure he was staying sober."

He stilled his automatic protest and forced himself to consider her words, which, damn it, were reasonable enough. At this point an idea struck him. "How about a bargain?"

"What bargain?" Her voice was wary.

"If you agree to finish checking out the other Nevada herds before you go on to the next state, then I'll agree to consider supervised visits here for the Jennings."

"Wait a sec. I have to agree to do it while you just have to agree to consider doing it. Unfair."

His lips twitched into a half-smile. "I never get to put anything over on you. That's unfair, too."

She shook her head. "We both plain agree or *nada*."

"You drive a hard bargain." No way was he going to tell her what a relief it was to come down off his hard-nosed stand. He'd thought of himself as a reasonable man, one to consider all angles—but he'd certainly been proven wrong today. He didn't much like the picture he'd presented.

"We'll try to explain to Sage," she said. "Do you think she'll be willing to listen?"

He shrugged. "We'll do our best."

"She not only loves you, she admires you," Laura told him.

"Not much to admire in what she heard today," he admitted.

"I said a few things I regret," she said ruefully.

He grinned at her, suddenly feeling lighthearted. "A couple of soreheads sniping at each other."

"Well, maybe."

"I can see you're all set to tell me it was my fault."

She shook her head, her lips twitching in an obviously repressed smile. "Never."

"Kiss and make up?"

"I'll go as far as a handshake."

He reached for her hand, holding it between both of his, feeling the ring she wore on her fourth finger. His ring. His wife. He wondered if she ever really would be.

Laura closed her eyes briefly, gathering her defenses, determined not to show him how much his slightest touch affected her. His fingers caressed hers, easing over her wedding ring, the ring that supposedly bound her to him. She swallowed, realizing how much she wanted to keep that ring on her hand.

"The hell with holding hands," he muttered, reaching for her and pulling her into his arms. For a moment before his mouth covered hers, she gazed into his dark, dark eyes, seeing a glow in them that made her catch her breath.

And then she was lost in the kiss that joined more than their lips. He held her heart to heart, making her fancy the two hearts beating as one, making them a part of each other.

She had no idea how much time passed before Grandfather's voice brought her out of her bemused state.

"See," he said, "I told you they'd make up and everything would be all right."

She and Shane broke apart hastily. Laura, seeing a wide-eyed Sage standing in the curve of Grandfather's arm, sprang up from the couch.

"I'm so sorry I upset you," she told the girl.

"You're going to leave," Sage muttered, leaning against Grandfather.

"I postponed my trip to Montana."

"And I'm not the total bad guy I sounded like," Shane put in. "Jennings and I are going to arrange for his family to come to the ranch once in a while so you can get to know the baby."

Sage eyed him dubiously. "Honest?"

"You do want to meet your other half brother, don't you?"

She nodded hesitantly.

"I didn't mean to make you feel bad," he said. "Are you ready to give me a hug?"

Sage burst into tears and flew into Shane's arms. When she finally got to the sniffling stage, Shane led her to the couch and motioned to Laura to sit down again, Sage sandwiched between them.

"You scared us," he told his sister. Looking at Grandfather, he said, "Are you going to let us know where you found her?"

The old man shook his head. "That's a secret between Sage and me."

Shane shook his head. "Figures."

Sage stared up at Laura. "You're not going to Montana?"

"Not for a while. I need to take a look at the other Nevada mustang herds first."

"But you're still going to leave sometime?"

Before Laura could speak, Shane said, "Laura and I have some things to discuss first, okay? By the way, did the colt get fed?"

Sage jumped up. "Poor Star!" she cried. "He'll think I don't love him anymore."

After she dashed from the room, Grandfather said to Shane, "Disposed of some of your ghosts, I see. About time."

Laura glanced from one to the other, not quite understanding. Ghosts?

"Didn't even need a fire," Shane said. Apparently seeing Laura's puzzlement, he added, "It comes from a story about Lonely-She-Walks."

"Grandfather told me that story, but what does it have to do with you?" she asked him.

"Jennings was my ghost. Not really him, but hating him."

"Hate eats at the spirit," Grandfather said. "Like

fear, when there's no reason to be afraid.'' He rose.
''I'm going to the barn. Maybe someone around
here will come up with an idea for supper pretty
soon. I missed my lunch.''

They'd all missed lunch, Laura realized, and it
was nearly five. She'd intended to go grocery shopping today because they were low on supplies. There
wasn't much left in the pantry to chose from. Beans,
she decided. Hot dogs and beans and a salad. ''Are
you up for cooking on the outside grill?'' she asked
Shane.

''Providing you make some more cookies—we're
all out.''

''Always trying to strike a bargain, aren't you? In
the interest of those in danger of starving to death,
I suppose I'll have to agree. But after we eat, we
need to get into the truck and head for Reno to stock
up for tomorrow—that's part of the bargain.''

Driving into Reno with Shane after dinner, Laura
said, ''What did you mean when you told Sage you
and I had things to discuss?''

''Since we're not going to discuss them until tomorrow, you'll find out then.''

''But I thought we were riding out to find the
bachelor herd tomorrow.''

''We are. How many bachelors did you spot in
that herd today?''

''Five. The same as before. Why?''

''One of them was a good size, looked older than
the others. Bigger anyway. You remember that bay

with the white splotches on his flanks? I figure he might be getting ready to make his move.''

''What move?''

''A challenge. He'll never get any mares otherwise.''

''You mean he'll try to take them away from the black stallion?''

Shane nodded. ''He has to fight him and win first.''

''Is that the only way a bachelor can ever get a mare?''

''Usually. Once in a while a mare will stray away from a ranch and hook up with a bachelor. And occasionally one'll get stolen from a harem by a sneaky loner.''

''You mean the mares aren't loyal to the stallion who keeps them in his harem?''

He shook his head. ''The poor guy is kept busy rounding them up. The more he collects, the harder he has to work to keep them all together.''

''I take it a harem of women is not your ideal.''

He slanted her a look. ''One woman at a time is sometimes too many.''

Laura decided not to touch that one. ''Should we take camping gear tomorrow?'' she asked.

''Best to. The herd may travel a distance between when you saw them this afternoon and tomorrow morning. Or we may not even spot them.''

She wouldn't admit it to him for the world, but she was looking forward to that night camp. They needed to be alone, without Grandfather or Sage. As

Shane had said, they needed to talk. And what else did they need?

Her body had told her what she needed quite clearly when she was wrapped in his arms on the couch earlier today. Laura sighed, feeling as though she'd been caught up in an unexpected torrent that was rushing her along a course she could neither predict nor change.

She found it frightening, but at the same time exhilarating—even if she didn't know where she'd wind up.

Chapter Fourteen

When they rode out the next morning rather late, Laura thought Shane seemed preoccupied. Which was okay with her, since she herself had more than enough to think about.

She was beginning to realize there was not going to be an easy way for her to ride off into the sunset. She couldn't bear to hurt Sage, for one thing. The girl really did need her. Glancing at Shane, she wondered how he felt about her leaving. As for her, part of her insisted it was the only way to avoid disaster, but, just the same, she no longer wanted to go.

She did have to finish documenting the condition of the western herds for the grant, which meant temporary stays in other states. After that, though—what?

Though she knew hearts didn't grow lighter or heavier, the sensation in her chest felt very much as though her heart was heavy. As if matching her mood, a cloud slid over the sun, making Laura look up at the sky.

"I thought you told me it didn't rain in the summer here," she said.

"Hardly ever does."

"Those look like rain clouds to me."

"We do get clouds, but it's so dry this time of the year that they dissipate."

"Well, okay, but if this was back east, we'd be heading for a thunderstorm."

"The mountains shape our weather. Most of the rainfall is on the California side. We get only what manages to make it over the peaks."

"You know, I never thought I'd come to appreciate this high desert country."

"So you told me before."

She shot him an annoyed glance. She might be repeating herself, but he didn't have to remind her.

To her right a covey of quail fluttered up from the sagebrush, landing almost immediately to hurry away on foot from the horses, their topknots quivering.

"It's amazing to me how many birds and animals live around here," she said. "It doesn't seem like there'd be enough to eat. And please don't point out who eats who."

She watched a reluctant smile tug at his mouth. "You don't want to hear about the food chain?"

"Supermarkets are food chains as far as I'm concerned."

That brought a chuckle from him. "Was it about here you spotted the bachelor herd yesterday?"

Laura nodded, pointing. "They were headed that way."

"In a hurry?"

"No, just sort of ambling along. That one white stallion really stands out."

"He's smaller than the rest. Might be some Arabian blood showing up like it does from time to time."

As they rode on, she realized Shane had been right about the clouds. They were thinning rather than thickening. Dissipating, as he'd said. He should be an area weather expert—after all he'd lived here all his life.

Roots. Somehow she'd failed to put down any, not even at her childhood home. Was it because they'd moved after that October?

Pushing that thought from her mind, Laura focused on Shane again and found him looking at her. "Grandfather dreamed last night," he said. "I heard about it this morning."

"One of what Sage calls his true dreams?"

"He thinks so. In his dream Coyote was trying to get into the house. He would have—the doors were wide open—if the palomino mare Grandfather saw in an earlier dream hadn't chased Coyote away. This was not *a* coyote, you understand, but the Trickster himself."

She nodded. "I think I'm supposed to be the palomino from that earlier dream, but I don't understand either that dream or this one. Or for that matter, the last dream I had."

"I'm not too sure about Grandfather's Coyote dream myself. He assures me it's a good omen. I hope so." The grimness darkening his last few words made her stare at him.

Was Shane's heart heavy, too?

"Coyote was in that piece of wood you were asking me about awhile back," he said. "I let him loose."

She knew he was talking about his carving, but didn't see what that had to do with Grandfather's dream.

"And I also finally saw what was in an odd-colored chunk I collected a couple years ago," he went on. "Could never make it out until yesterday."

"Does that happen often? That it takes years for you to tell what you want to carve out of a particular piece of wood?"

"Once in awhile."

"I'm afraid you having had to shepherd me around has put you behind in your carving."

"Some," he admitted.

His answer wasn't exactly to her liking. What had she expected him to say? she asked herself. That being with her was worth it?

He checked his horse as he examined the ground, so she slowed, too.

"Some mustangs passed this way," he said.

"Could be the bachelors." He scanned the sweep of land.

She followed his gaze and saw nothing moving. Certainly no wild horses.

"Best to keep fairly close to the stream," he said. "We'll be camping near it tonight if we don't locate the herd in the next couple of hours."

She glanced up to check on the clouds. Still there, but now with gaps in between. Overhead, a hawk soared in a thermal, spiraling higher and higher.

"I never understood how hawks can possibly spot prey from way up there," she said.

"I thought what eats what was taboo talk."

She made a face at him.

He grinned at her, the weight in his chest easing some. The solid conviction that if he didn't pull it off tonight it'd be too late, had plagued him since late yesterday. That was one of the reasons he'd spent half the night carving. For what he'd seen in that strange-colored chunk was part of his scheme, and he'd needed to finish carving the animal in order to put it to use.

What if his plan didn't work?

Shane shook his head. It damn well had to. Otherwise they'd both lose their chance to stay together.

A while later they stopped to rest their horses and have something to eat. They were on their way again when he was alerted by a faint sound carried on the wind that had risen, as usual, in the afternoon. Shane halted the gelding and swiveled his head from side to side, trying to pinpoint the sound.

"Do you hear anything?" he asked Laura.

She tilted her head to listen, then frowned. "Did someone—something—scream? It sounds pretty far away."

"Stallion challenge," he said. Satisfied where the noise was coming from, he prodded Cloud into a trot. "Stay behind me. We may have to stop in a hurry."

The screams grew louder as they approached a rise. He slowed the gelding as they climbed, halting him short of the crest and dismounting. "Do what I do," he told Laura. "Our horses won't spook them, but we might."

He led Cloud at an angle up to the top, using the horse to conceal him, just as the mare blocked most of Laura. Below them he saw one of the most dramatic of all mustang scenes. Beside him he heard Laura draw in her breath.

The black stallion, ears laid back, snorting, faced the bachelor bay stallion with the white flank spots. Off to the side the mares, several foals and the yearling, huddled together awaiting the outcome. There was no sign of the other bachelor stallions.

The bay, his ears flat against his head, screamed, and, baring his teeth, rushed toward the black. The black whirled and bumped against his side, staggering him. Then the black rose on hind legs and struck at the bay with his forelegs. He connected and the bay gave ground.

Swinging around, he did his best to kick the black. The black slid around and bit him in the neck.

"Oh my, he drew blood," Laura whispered.

"They both mean business."

"One wouldn't actually kill the other would he?"

"It's been known to happen," he said. "Usually the loser backs off in time to save his life."

Laura grabbed his hand and hung on. "I don't want to see this, but I can't look away," she said.

The stallions' screams pierced the desert air as they lunged at one another, kicking, biting, and slamming into each other. Just as it seemed clear the bay was losing, Laura pulled her hand away and pointed.

"Look over there," she told him.

Shane did. On the far side of the group of mares, the white stallion had appeared from nowhere and was quietly separating a pinto mare from the rest. As the gap widened between her and the other mares, she turned and obediently trotted off with the white stallion.

By the time the fight between the two stallions wound down the pair was almost out of sight. The bay, clearly defeated and not wanting any more punishment, sidled away. The black kept feinting at him until finally the bay whirled and trotted off, leaving the black still head of his harem. He immediately rounded up the mares, and chivvied them off in the opposite direction.

"That was the most awesome sight I've ever watched," Laura said.

"Not much beats a fight between two stallions."

"The black didn't seem to realize his harem had

been reduced,'' she went on. ''The nerve of that white stallion sneaking off with one of those mares while the bay was doing the fighting. It doesn't seem fair that the white got a reward while the bay got nothing but a bunch of cuts and bites.''

''Haven't you heard the old saying—all's fair in love and war? The direct approach isn't always the most effective.''

Laura remained silent as they eased back down from the rise and remounted. As they rode away, she said, ''That's the slant the Paiute stories take, isn't it? Indirect. They cloak proper behavior and advice in tales.''

''Pretty much.''

''Will the bay rejoin the bachelor herd?''

He nodded, glad she changed the subject. The time wasn't ripe for the telling of tales. ''The losers usually do,'' he told her. ''Horses are herd animals. Safety in numbers.''

''But the white stallion and his mare are on their own, making three herds now, right?''

''You got it.''

''I'd like to catch up to the bachelor herd so I can make sure the bay wasn't seriously injured,'' she said. ''Is that possible, do you think?''

''They'll likely head for water. We'll camp and try.''

''Good.''

Exactly the way he felt. He needed that night camp.

By the time he located a suitable site near the

creek, the clouds had mostly dispersed, leaving a few that promised to make the sunset spectacular. He hadn't brought the tent since she hadn't used it since the first camp-out. Laura was as basic a camper as he was, something he never would've believed at their first meeting.

Come to that, he never would've believed he'd one day be inviting Jennings to his place. Goes to prove a man doesn't know as much as he thinks he does. Grandfather always said a person who stopped learning was one of the walking dead.

Shane knew who had made him learn. Laura. She was responsible for changing his outlook, for teaching him how to love. Now it was his turn to teach her, if he could, that to love doesn't bring disaster.

"I'll never forget seeing those stallions fight," she said over their evening meal. "I didn't realize horses could inflict so much damage on one another."

He shrugged. "Men fight over women—why shouldn't stallions fight over mares?"

"I'm talking about wild mustangs," she said. "Men are supposed to be civilized."

"We try to be, but most of us are as wild at heart as those mustangs. Once in a while that wildness cuts loose."

"When I first met you—" she began, but didn't finish.

"What about it?"

"Um, well, I compared you in my mind to the black stallion."

Her words both startled and pleased him. "And now?"

"At least you don't have a harem," she said, smiling. After a moment or two she added, "In a way, though, you possess the same free spirit. I envy that."

"What if I were a black stallion," he said, "and you were the dream palomino mare. Would you be willing to roam the desert with me, the two of us galloping in the wind together?"

"In a minute," she said. "Because if I were that palomino, I'd be as free-spirited as you, with no doubts and no fears." She sighed. "Wouldn't it be wonderful?"

He nodded.

She helped him clean up after they finished eating and then they sat near the dying fire on sleeping bags, both staring at the red coals.

If he intended to carry through with his plan, he'd better get to it before the fire went completely out. He rose, saying, "I've got something for you."

Retrieving the basket from his gear, he walked back to the fire and handed it to her. Laura took it, gazing questioningly at him.

"You're not to take the lid off yet," he said.

She examined the basket in the uncertain light. "It's beautiful."

"My great-grandmother made it."

"And you want me to have this priceless basket?"

"Yes. It has to be yours."

"I don't know what to say—thank you seems inadequate for a work of art."

"Now that you've acknowledged this burden basket as yours, please hand it back to me."

When she did, Shane carefully removed the lid and set it aside. He reached into the basket, pulled his closed hand out and opened it over the coals.

Laura, suddenly feeling as though she was reliving her strange dream, stared at him blankly. Though she'd seen nothing drop from his hand, she finally asked, "Did you throw something in the fire?"

"Yes," he said, repeating the action. "Here goes another one."

"There wasn't anything in your hand," she said, trying to remain logical, which was difficult with her dream closing in around her.

"Ghosts are invisible." Two more times he disposed of what she couldn't see and felt sure he couldn't either—neither of them could see. With the last, the coals sizzled and crackled as though actually consuming something, just as in her dream.

"Now that all four ghosts are gone, it's time for you to take out what remains inside," he told her, handing the basket back to her.

Warily, her gaze fixed on him, she thrust her hand into the basket. "Oh, there is something!" she cried, bringing it into view.

There was just enough light left to see the green of the carving as Laura held it in her hands. Shane wondered why, with the wood that odd greenish shade, he hadn't seen that it held *pamogo* until last evening.

"Oh, Shane," she whispered, "you carved a frog for me." Her voice broke on the last word and tears shone in her eyes as she cuddled the wooden frog to her.

"It's my gift to you. Now that we've disposed of the ghosts, you're free to love Pamogo, your very own Paiute frog. As well as his carver."

Tears running down her cheeks, she laid the frog carefully back into the basket. He put the lid on the basket and lifted it away.

"Let me hold you while you tell me what the ghosts of the past were," he murmured, sounding more positive than he felt.

He'd done what he could, the rest was up to her.

Laura gazed at Shane through her tears. Tell him? How could she tell anyone? Yet hadn't he burned her ghosts in the fire like in the dream Grandfather had told her to remember? Did she want to be Lonely-She-Walks for the rest of her life?

She edged closer to him, and he pulled her against him, her back to his chest. The right position to tell him, she realized, because she couldn't bear to look at him while she spoke.

"It was Halloween," she said, feeling a wave of fear pass through her as she conjured up that terrible night. "Nathan and I went trick-or-treating. We were supposed to stay together, but I hated feeling like a baby with my big brother having to take me around.

"I saw some friends of mine across the street and, while Nathan was talking to a couple of his friends, I started to sneak over to join them. Before I got all the way across, a car stopped and a man called my name."

Laura swallowed before she could go on. "I knew all about strangers in cars, but he wasn't a stranger, he was Daddy's partner, the man I called Uncle Clint, the man who sometimes brought me treats and who told me how pretty I was. I liked Uncle Clint a lot. He wasn't a stranger.

"'Laurie,' he said. Nobody else called me that. 'I've been looking for you because I have a real treat for you. Get in and you can have it.' So I did."

She clenched her fists, forcing herself to go on, beginning to feel like the terror-stricken child she'd been then. "Uncle Clint drove off real fast, and he began saying all these strange things, like how I was going to be his little girl now and how I'd never see Mama and Daddy again. 'Serve the bastard right,' he kept muttering.

"I told him I wanted to go home, and he laughed and said our home was going to be in Mexico, that's where we were headed and wouldn't I like to be a little Mexican señorita? He didn't act at all like the Uncle Clint I knew—he'd turned into a stranger.

"So then I knew that I'd done a bad thing—I'd gotten into a car with a stranger, after all. He wasn't the nice, kind man I was so fond of."

She paused, trying to find words to go on.

"So right then you decided it wasn't safe to ever

be fond of anyone or anything again," Shane said softly, almost into her ear.

She nodded. "Something terrible would happen. Like what happened with Uncle Clint."

"What did happen?"

"He drove and drove. I found a way to hide inside my mind so I could stop thinking. Finally he stopped and I didn't want to get out, but he hauled me from the car and when I recognized where we were I got scared all over again. It was his cottage by the lake—we'd been there lots of times in the summers. I began to cry when he brought me inside, so then he made me swallow something that tasted awful, and I got dizzy and sick, and then I started to fall asleep.

"All the time he kept moving around, talking, talking, telling me how he was going to be my new daddy and take me to Mexico where we'd never be found. I was afraid to go to sleep, but I couldn't help it."

She unclenched her hands. "When I woke up I was awful sick and threw up and somehow Mama was there and Daddy was muttering about 'that son of a bitch Clint' and so I knew it'd been real and not a bad dream."

"How did they rescue you?" Shane's breath was warm on her ear.

She began to relax, leaning into him. "Nathan saw me get into the car and recognized Uncle Clint. He'd overheard Daddy that morning say he was going to have to call the cops about his partner, so he ran home and told our folks what had happened. Daddy did call the police then and told them where Clint lived and about the cottage and they found me. I didn't even know I'd been rescued because the drug he'd given me made me sleep all through it.''

She turned around and clung to Shane, leaning against his chest as she told him what had troubled her all her life. ''Nobody told me what happened to Uncle Clint, but I saw on the TV news about how he'd put a pistol in his mouth and pulled the trigger when the police drove up to the cottage. He killed himself, and it was my fault.''

''No way,'' Shane told her. ''No child is responsible for a man killing himself.''

She raised her head. ''But if I hadn't gotten into his car—''

''That has nothing to do with his suicide. Why was your father intending to turn his partner in? Embezzlement?''

''Something like that. He cheated Daddy. I didn't ever want to learn the details.''

''Ghosts of the past,'' Shane said, ''made you cling to your child's reasoning. Think about it.''

She gazed into his eyes, seeing the warmth and concern. Taking a deep breath, she tried to order her mind to coherent thought. ''If I hadn't liked Uncle Clint, I wouldn't've got into his car,'' she said finally. ''If I hadn't gotten into the car, he wouldn't have scared me. And he wouldn't have killed himself.''

Shane nodded. "That's how little Laura reasoned. But you're no longer a child."

His words settled over her like a balm. She was an adult, not a child. Why was she still thinking like one? Remembering all her hours of therapy as a teenager, she realized that if she'd been able to bring herself to talk about that Halloween to the therapist as honestly as she had to Shane, she might have led an entirely different life.

But then she wouldn't have met Shane. He was the one who'd found a way to burn her ghosts in the fire. He was the only man in the world she could ever love.

She reached up with both hands and pulled his head down until their lips met.

At that moment a chorus of coyote wails drifted on the evening breeze. Shane broke the kiss long enough to murmur, "That's applause, you know."

If anyone had ever told her she'd be sitting in a desert camp, listening to coyotes, while hoping a man with a wild heart would make love to her, she wouldn't have believed a word of it.

But her dream hadn't ended this way. Her dream had ended with Shane walking away from her. He could still do that. Except in the dream she hadn't told him about the past. So this wasn't the same.

Wrapping her arms tightly around him, she found his lips again, putting all she felt in her heart into her kiss.

Chapter Fifteen

Unsure at first whether Laura was merely seeking consolation in a kiss, Shane leashed his passion, waiting for a clear signal. When she began to unbutton his shirt, he decided she had something else entirely in mind. Exactly the same thing he did.

He shucked off the shirt and reached for her again. Before he gathered her to him, she managed to pull off her T-shirt, surprising him, sending a flare of desire into his loins.

"There's never going to be anything between us," she whispered against his lips. "Not anymore."

Joy blazing through him, he murmured, "In that case, we've still got too many clothes on."

Their lips met in a slow, hot kiss. He meant to

keep everything slow, to savor every inch of her, but it was soon clear from the way she tugged at his belt buckle that she had other ideas. A quick and eager learner, this beautiful and passionate woman who was his wife.

Yielding to her insistence, he flung the rest of his clothes aside, at the same time watching her shed everything she wore, wishing the moon was full so he could appreciate the sweet curves of her body. He wanted to see as well as touch as she stretched out on the sleeping bag beside him.

She ran her hand over his abdomen, her caress making his muscles contract as her fingers dipped lower. He groaned as she found his arousal. Her inexperience increased his pleasure.

Shane seemed to like her touching him, Laura told herself as she explored his masculinity. She doubted if she'd ever tire of seeing him naked, of caressing him everywhere. She found his body beautiful.

"Whoa," he said huskily. "Take it easy, honey. Let me have my turn before it's too late."

He began nuzzling her breasts, taking first one, then the other into his mouth, making heat coil in her lower abdomen until she began to ache with longing. When his lips finally met hers again, she wriggled her body against him, the feel of his warm skin against hers driving her wild with need.

His kiss deepened, so that she could taste his flavor, enticing, erotic. His hands explored her body with intimate caresses that made her moan with pleasure. The scent of sage crushed by the sleeping bags rose around them, and the smell seemed so right. Was right.

Just as their lovemaking was right.

And then he eased into her and all thought fled, replaced by the indescribably wonderful sensations that were a part of their love for one another. Again they traveled a wildfire path of passion neither could have found without each other.

She snuggled against him afterward, warm and content. "This is so wonderful," she murmured.

"It's always going to be this good," he told her, "because I'm always going to love you. I can't say nothing bad will ever happen, but if it does, we'll face it together."

"I know. You burned the ghosts. It's all right for me to love you. Even if it wasn't, though, I couldn't help myself."

"So you admit we were meant for each other, after all."

"You said yourself Grandfather is usually right."

Shane raised himself on one elbow. "Did he tell you we were made for each other?"

"Not directly. You know Grandfather. But when I look back, it was clear from the beginning that I was his pick for his grandson to marry. And not just for Sage's sake, either."

"What can I say? We Bearclaws have good taste when it comes to women."

She poked him in the ribs, discovered he was ticklish, and their playful wrestling turned into something else, something timeless and wonderful.

* * *

Shane woke abruptly near dawn, finding himself zipped into their joined sleeping bags with Laura. He lay quietly, listening for what had awoken him and heard the soft whuffle of a horse. Cloud, greeting other horses. Which meant the wild ones were near.

"Mustang alert," he whispered into Laura's ear. "Wake up."

She opened her eyes, blue as the Nevada sky.

"Don't move quickly," he warned. Easing onto one elbow he bent and brushed his lips over hers in a good morning kiss.

Cautiously sitting up, he peered through the cottonwoods in the uncertain predawn light and saw the white-spotted bay, yesterday's loser. Three other stallions trailed behind him, all heading for the creek.

"The bachelor herd," he whispered to Laura who'd eased up beside him.

He counted four—only the white stallion who'd stolen the mare was missing. The bay didn't look too badly hurt—he wasn't bleeding.

They sat unmoving while the mustangs advanced to the creek and drank their fill. Only when the bay began circling Colly, the mare, did Shane haul himself free of the sleeping bag.

"You can't have that one, *pooggoo*," he called. "Better luck with the black next time."

Long before he finished, the mustangs were racing away, tails flying.

"I love to see them run," Laura said, standing beside him. "What's that word you called the bay?"

"Our word for horse."

"He seemed in pretty good shape considering how violent that battle looked. I guess it's a case of 'he who fights and runs away, lives to fight another day.'"

"You don't have any clothes on," he told her.

"My dear sir, neither do you. Whatever shall we do about it?"

He pulled her into his arms, murmuring, "I'll think of something."

Much later, mounted on his gelding, Shane, with Laura beside him on the mare, headed home.

"Would the mare have gone with the bay if she hadn't been tethered?" she asked.

He nodded. "The gelding, too, possibly. The mustang stallions are always trying to steal mares wherever they can, and geldings also can feel the call of the wild."

"The mustangs don't mind geldings joining them?"

"Even stallions with harems have been known to tolerate stray geldings."

"Interesting that they realize a gelding is no competition," she said. "So, anyway, I'll be reporting three herds on the reservation. Will the black stallion accept the white one being on his range now that the white's starting his own harem?"

"With some posturing and feinting if they happen to meet, probably. My take is the white'll steer clear of him as much as he can."

They discussed horses for most of the ride back home. A smug-looking Sage met them at the corral. Though her expression made Shane a bit suspicious, he was glad to see she no longer seemed upset.

"What's up?" he asked, as he dismounted and caught Laura as she slid off.

"How come you're not letting go of her?" Sage asked.

"I like the way she feels. You didn't answer my question."

"Grandfather and I have been invited to a barbecue," Sage told him. "You and Laura, too."

"When and where?" he asked.

"Tonight. I told them we'd all come."

Shane frowned. "You couldn't be sure we'd be back."

"I could, too. Grandfather said you would."

"Where is the barbecue?" Laura asked.

"At somebody's ranch over in Carson Valley. Jade said you'd know how to get there 'cause you were there before."

Shane looked at Laura. "So where are we going?"

"It must be Zed Adams's ranch. Remember, I mentioned him before—one of Jade's brothers."

"Yeah, Zed's the name Jade told me," Sage interrupted. "We can come any time after five. Grandfather's looking forward to it. So'm I."

Laura looked up at him, and Shane bent and kissed her, forgetting for the moment where they were.

"Whoa, that's more like it," Sage said. "Want me to take care of the horses while you guys go in and change clothes?"

When she got to her bedroom, Laura was surprised to find the dresser top empty of her belongings. She opened a drawer and found it bare. She was heading for the closet to look inside when she heard Shane call her.

"Come here a minute, Laura."

Hurrying into his room, she gasped. On top of his double dresser lay her brush, her makeup kit and her other things. Shane opened a drawer and held up one of her bikini panties.

"And your clothes have joined mine in the closet," he added.

"Well, I admit I was seriously considering moving in," she admitted, "but no one knew that except maybe you."

"Grandfather."

She raised her eyebrows.

"Ten to one he told Sage to move your stuff."

Staring at Shane, she said, "How could he possibly have known?"

"He's as wily as they come, that old *poohaguma*."

"Dare I ask what that means?"

"Medicine man. He'll take credit for the entire affair, wait and see."

Laura started to laugh. After a moment Shane joined her, and soon they both collapsed onto the bed, laughing so hard tears came to her eyes. He pulled her close and kissed her and one thing led to another until she finally pulled away.

"I didn't think to close the door," she said breathlessly. "Anyway, it's after four. We'd better shower and change for the barbecue."

"Together?"

Seeing the glow in his eyes, she couldn't refuse.

Considering everything, Laura thought it remarkable that they all were in the extended cab pickup and on their way by five-fifteen.

She felt dazed, as though she were existing in a dream state, a pleasant sensation, and she wondered if it happened to everyone who fell in love with the right person.

"Does Zed have any kids?" Sage asked from the back seat.

Coming back to reality, Laura thought a minute, then said, "Yes, two at last count. Jade and Nathan have Tim, so that's at least three kids who'll be there. If Zed's brother is home, there'll be three more."

"Good. I hate being the only one," Sage said.

"You'll be the oldest of all the kids, though."

"That's okay. My teacher last year said I was a

good organizer. Maybe I'll teach them some games and stuff.''

''If Jade brought her guitar we'll probably all wind up singing folk songs,'' Laura said.

Shane thought most likely he'd enjoy the evening. Barbecues were held outside, which meant he'd be free to wander around. He and Laura's brother might not yet be buddies, but Nate was no longer hostile, which would go a long way toward making the others accept him as Laura's husband, no matter how rushed and secret the marriage might have seemed to them.

When he finally reached the ranch driveway Laura pointed out to him, he pulled in, noting with interest that there seemed to be quite a few cars and trucks already parked near the ranch house. More than family had been invited apparently.

''It looks like there's lots of people here,'' Sage piped up. ''Maybe there'll be some kids my age, after all.''

They piled out of the truck and started toward the sound of voices and laughter. Two boys chasing one another were the first to see them.

''Hey, Danny, that's Laura and Shane,'' the dark-haired one called, changing course to intercept them. Tim, Shane saw.

Both boys ran up. ''Hi, I'm Danny,'' the sandy-haired one said, staring at Grandfather, who had his hair in two braids, as usual.

"I'm Grandfather," the old man said. He put his hand on Sage's shoulder. "And this is Sage."

"You're her grandfather?" Danny asked.

"Everyone calls me Grandfather," he said. "It's the name I like best."

Danny nodded. "Okay. Come on, I'll show you where my mom and dad are."

"Oh, there's Linnea," Laura said as they neared a laughing group of people. "Talal must be back. He's Jade's other brother."

A blond woman approached and hugged Laura. "I'm Karen, Zed's wife," she said, looking from Shane to Grandfather.

Danny began pointing. "He's Shane and she's Sage and he's Grandfather. That's what he wants to be called. He told me so."

"I'm so glad you're here," Karen said. "Danny, why don't you take Sage to meet the other kids?"

"Okay." He turned to Sage. "Except for Tim and me and Yasmin, they're pretty much babies," he told her.

Once Sage went off with Danny, Karen took the three of them in tow and made the rounds, introducing them. When they came to Gert Severin, Grandfather detached himself, saying to Gert, "You may be a kindred spirit."

She smiled at him. "If that proves to be true, we'll both be the richer."

Karen stopped beside a man she introduced as her brother, Steve, telling him to take Shane to the barn so he could meet Zed. "All the guys gather there," she added.

Laura, she led off and, collecting Linnea, Victoria and Jade, she claimed she needed help in the kitchen.

Laura knew Victoria was Steve's wife, having met her when she and Steve were married, so she suspected this family gathering of wives had a hidden purpose. She soon discovered she was right.

"Didn't I tell you?" Jade asked, as soon as they were more or less private in the kitchen. "Shane's some hunk, isn't he?"

"He *is* gorgeous," Victoria agreed. "Where did you meet him, Laura?"

"Actually, he literally swept me off my feet and onto his horse," Laura told them, enjoying the sensation of knowing her man intrigued them.

"You're kidding," Linnea said.

Laura shook her head and launched into a brief explanation. She didn't mention why they'd married. Some day she might confess to Jade, but not now. They seemed to believe she'd married for love—which is how it had turned out to be.

"I don't blame you for nabbing him right on the spot," Jade said. "Still, we all felt a tad left out, since we missed the wedding. So we decided to get together and have an informal reception for you and Shane. Mostly family, but with a few guests who feel like family."

Laura stared at her. "You mean—tonight?"

Karen nodded. "But you don't get to open the presents until later. First we eat."

Blinking back tears, Laura tried to thank them all. At that moment Sage came in with a little red-haired toddler by the hand.

Steve and Victoria's Heidi, as it turned out.

"You have to come see the twins," Sage told Laura. "They're so cute."

Moments later, as Laura found herself surrounded by children of all ages—though none as old as Sage—it came to her that part of loving a man was wanting his child.

Later, after everyone had eaten, Karen shooed Laura and Shane off, insisting they take a stroll to the gazebo before the grand finale of opening presents. "It's a tradition," Karen said. "Most of us did it before we got married, but we'll make an exception for you two."

She pointed them in the right direction and, hand in hand, Laura and Shane walked toward the side garden.

"You didn't tell me Zed and Talal were twins," he said. "Took me a while to get used to who was which. I'd've married you even sooner if I'd known what a great extended family you have. Talal wants to donate some money to our fishery, and Zed's all set to take my scout troop on a camel ride."

"I didn't realize how accepted I was. Do you know Steve and Victoria flew all the way from Virginia so they could be here for our reception?"

"You didn't mind Gert being invited?"

She shook her head and smiled at him. "Not now that I can look at her as a possible friend instead of a shrink."

"She and Grandfather must operate on the same wavelength. I've been told she's coming out to visit us—him, really. Seems she's fascinated by how Native American medicine men successfully treat mental problems in their own cultures."

"They make an interesting combination."

"A dangerous one. If Gert knows even half as much as Grandfather, we all better watch out."

The sweet scent of roses surrounded them as they came to the gazebo. The moon, fading toward its dark period, cast little light, but the crescent rode high among the stars.

"A gazebo might be nice down by the honeysuckle," she said dreamily. "The children could play in it."

He stopped and put his hands on her shoulders. "You mean Sage and her friends?"

"They're getting a little old for that. I was thinking of—ours."

Shane closed his eyes for a moment, overwhelmed by the wave of feeling that broke over him. Their children. His and Laura's. Opening his eyes, he gazed down at her upturned face. To him, the most beautiful face in the world.

"Aren't we lucky we found each other?" she asked.

He nodded. "But I'm still not completely sure that somehow Grandfather didn't have a hand in it."

She laughed. "I don't care if he did. I love him, too. And Sage. And, right now, the whole world. But especially you."

Shane drew her close and kissed her, knowing however it had happened, he'd love this woman until the end of time.

Chapter Sixteen

Because the last of the New Mexico wild horses were rounded up and shipped out of the state before she was to go there, Laura completed her grant work sooner than she'd expected. On a sunny Saturday in late November, she leaned against the corral fence, watching as Sage led the gangly Star around the enclosure with a halter.

"He's quit fighting it," Sage called to her.

"That's because he trusts you," Laura said, thinking privately that Star would follow the girl wherever she led, do anything she wanted him to.

"I'm glad he's mine, but sometimes I'm sorry he can't run free like the other mustangs."

Laura smiled, thinking of Shane. She was glad *he* was hers, but she couldn't say she was sorry he wasn't running free.

She heard the pickup pull into the drive and stop. Grandfather was back from Tourmaline. He'd spent several days there visiting Gert Severin so she knew he'd be in good spirits. The sound of distant hammering told her Shane was still working down by the garden.

"Mail's here," Grandfather announced, coming into view. "Seems to be a letter here from some strange place in the Middle East."

"Kholi!" Sage cried and came running over, halter forgotten, the colt trailing her anyway.

"Didn't say it was for you," Grandfather teased, as she held out her hand.

Zed, Talal and Jade's grandmother had visited from Kholi in the fall, bringing with her two grandnephews. The younger one, Tabuk, was twelve. Sage's way with Star had impressed Tabuk—a girl actually training a colt! Unheard of in his country. He was also interested in her Native American heritage, finding it comparable to his own Bedouin ancestry. So he and Sage had become friends. Now that he'd returned to Kholi they were pen pals.

"Tabuk says his father has agreed he can go to the University of Nevada at Reno when he's eighteen," Sage reported, scanning the letter. "He'll be right here in Reno—isn't that great?"

Laura reasoned that Tabuk's father wanted Talal to keep an eye on the boy and that might well be why UNR had been chosen. In the meantime, she thought it was great that Sage could enjoy this long-distance friendship.

"Look, he sent me a picture." Sage waved it in the air. "Isn't he way cool? Donna's going to just die."

All the Zohir men Laura had met were handsome, and Tabuk was no exception. "He's a good-looking boy," she agreed.

Handing over the letter and picture to her, Sage said, "I'm going to put it in a frame like I did little Joey's."

"Joey's cute, too," Laura said smiling.

"Yeah, but he's only a baby and my baby brother besides. Tabuk's different." Sage turned to Star who was nuzzling her shoulder and threw her arms around his neck. Laura smiled. She wouldn't have to start really worrying about Sage and boys for a few years yet.

As for Joey, Shane's change of heart had been good for all of them. He'd tolerated Bill and Connie's visit with the baby surprisingly well. It boded well for a continuing relationship even though she knew Shane and Bill would never really be friends.

Returning to the house to put Sage's letter in her room, Laura found the phone ringing. "We've done it!" her brother cried when she answered. "Anna Isabel, eight pounds, three ounces, mother and child in great shape."

Tears of joy in her eyes, Laura offered her sincere congratulations. After Jade's miscarriage, they'd wanted this baby so desperately.

"Tim is as excited as we are," Nathan added before hanging up.

Laura smiled as she left the house by the front door, taking the path toward the garden. Toward Shane.

He stopped his carpentry work when he saw her coming, holding out his arms for her to walk into. After his bear hug, she told him about Anna Isabel.

"That's good news," he said.

They talked about Nathan and Jade for a few minutes, and then he gestured toward the half-built structure and asked, "What do you think?"

"I think it's going to be the most fantastic gazebo ever built, and it'll put every other one to shame."

He grinned at her. "If I ever get it finished, you mean."

"Oh, I expect you've got time enough."

He raised an eyebrow. "Time enough for what?"

"To get it done before He-Who-Is-Coming arrives."

Shane stared into her eyes, and she saw the dawning joy in his. "Are you—?"

She nodded. "And, since Grandfather had one of his true dreams last night, he very kindly told me it's a boy."

"He didn't know you were pregnant?"

"If you mean had I told him—no. But there's never any way of telling for sure what he knows or doesn't know. He says we'll have to wait until he dreams the right name before we can even think about what we want to call the baby."

"Do you mind?"

Laura shook her head. "No. Grandfather makes

me feel we're all safe somehow. Watched over. Which I suppose is foolish of me.''

"No more foolish than marrying me in the first place.''

Suppressing a smile, she said, ''It was purely a business arrangement.''

"That's what I thought. All I wanted was a woman in the house so I could keep Sage and look what happened.''

"I hear love's like that—sneaking up when you're not looking and zap, you're trapped. I tried to stay out of your bed, but—''

"That written agreement was doomed before the ink was dry,'' he told her, pulling her back into his arms.

"With Grandfather and Love with a capital L opposing me,'' she murmured, ''what chance did I have?''

His kiss showed her that, from the moment they'd met, she was meant to be right where she was. In his arms, loving and loved, and free of the past forever.

* * * * *

Silhouette Romance is
proud to announce the
exciting continuation of

This time, Thorton royal
family secrets are exposed!

A Royal Masquerade
by Arlene James (#1432)
On sale March 2000

A Royal Marriage
by Cara Colter (#1440)
On sale April 2000

A Royal Mission
by Elizabeth August (#1446)
On sale May 2000

Available at your favorite retail outlet.

Where love comes alive™

Visit us at www.romance.net
SSERW2

If you enjoyed what you just read,
then we've got an offer you can't resist!

Take 2 bestselling
love stories FREE!
Plus get a FREE surprise gift!

Clip this page and mail it to Silhouette Reader Service™

IN U.S.A.	IN CANADA
3010 Walden Ave.	P.O. Box 609
P.O. Box 1867	Fort Erie, Ontario
Buffalo, N.Y. 14240-1867	L2A 5X3

YES! Please send me 2 free Silhouette Special Edition® novels and my free surprise gift. Then send me 6 brand-new novels every month, which I will receive months before they're available in stores. In the U.S.A., bill me at the bargain price of $3.80 plus 25¢ delivery per book and applicable sales tax, if any*. In Canada, bill me at the bargain price of $4.21 plus 25¢ delivery per book and applicable taxes**. That's the complete price and a savings of at least 10% off the cover prices—what a great deal! I understand that accepting the 2 free books and gift places me under no obligation ever to buy any books. I can always return a shipment and cancel at any time. Even if I never buy another book from Silhouette, the 2 free books and gift are mine to keep forever. So why not take us up on our invitation. You'll be glad you did!

235 SEN C224
335 SEN C225

Name	(PLEASE PRINT)	
Address	Apt.#	
City	State/Prov.	Zip/Postal Code

* Terms and prices subject to change without notice. Sales tax applicable in N.Y.
** Canadian residents will be charged applicable provincial taxes and GST.
   All orders subject to approval. Offer limited to one per household.
   ® are registered trademarks of Harlequin Enterprises Limited.

SPED00   ©1998 Harlequin Enterprises Limited

Multi-*New York Times* bestselling author

NORA ROBERTS

knew from the first how to capture readers' hearts.
Celebrate the 20th Anniversary of Silhouette Books
with this special 2-in-1 edition containing her fabulous
first book and the sensational sequel.

Coming in June

IRISH HEARTS

Adelia Cunnane's fiery temper sets proud, powerful horse
breeder Travis Grant's heart aflame and he resolves to
make this wild ***Irish Thoroughbred*** his own.

Erin McKinnon accepts wealthy Burke Logan's loveless
proposal, but can this ravishing ***Irish Rose*** win her
hard-hearted husband's love?

Also available in June from
Silhouette Special Edition (SSE #1328)

IRISH REBEL

In this brand-new sequel to ***Irish Thoroughbred***, Travis and
Adelia's innocent but strong-willed daughter Keeley discovers
love in the arms of a charming Irish rogue with a talent for
horses...and romance.

Silhouette®

Where love comes alive™

Visit Silhouette at www.eHarlequin.com   PSNORA

Attention Silhouette Readers:

Romance is just one click away!

online book **serials**

➤ *Exclusive* to our web site, get caught up in both the daily and weekly online installments of new romance stories.

➤ Try the Writing Round Robin. Contribute a chapter to a story created by our members. Plus, winners will get prizes.

romantic **travel**

➤ Want to know where the best place to kiss in New York City is, or which restaurant in Los Angeles is the most romantic? Check out our Romantic Hot Spots for the scoop.

➤ Share your travel tips and stories with us on the romantic travel message boards.

romantic reading **library**

➤ Relax as you read our collection of Romantic Poetry.

➤ Take a peek at the Top 10 Most Romantic Lines!

Visit us online at

www.eHarlequin.com

on Women.com Networks

SEUT1

**Coming soon from
Silhouette Special Edition**

A sensuous new miniseries from bestselling author

Susan Mallery
Desert Rogues

Meet Khalil, Jamal and Malik—strong, sexy,
impossibly stubborn sheik princes who do as they
see fit. But they'd better watch out, for life in the
royal palace is about to change forever when they
each claim a tempestuous American bride!

Escape to El Bahar—a majestic land where
seduction rules and romantic fantasies come alive....

THE SHEIK'S KIDNAPPED BRIDE
(SE #1316, on sale April 2000)

THE SHEIK'S ARRANGED MARRIAGE
(SE #1324, on sale May 2000)

THE SHEIK'S SECRET BRIDE
(SE #1331, on sale June 2000)

Desert Rogues:

Will passions flare for these brothers
under the hot desert sun?

Available at your favorite retail outlet.

Silhouette®
Where love comes alive™

Visit us at www.romance.net

SSEDR

SILHOUETTE'S 20ᵀᴴ ANNIVERSARY CONTEST
OFFICIAL RULES
NO PURCHASE NECESSARY TO ENTER

1. To enter, follow directions published in the offer to which you are responding. Contest begins 1/1/00 and ends on 8/24/00 (the "Promotion Period"). Method of entry may vary. Mailed entries must be postmarked by 8/24/00, and received by 8/31/00.

2. During the Promotion Period, the Contest may be presented via the Internet. Entry via the Internet may be restricted to residents of certain geographic areas that are disclosed on the Web site. To enter via the Internet, if you are a resident of a geographic area in which Internet entry is permissible, follow the directions displayed on-line, including typing your essay of 100 words or fewer telling us "Where In The World Your Love Will Come Alive." On-line entries must be received by 11:59 p.m. Eastern Standard time on 8/24/00. Limit one e-mail entry per person, household and e-mail address per day, per presentation. If you are a resident of a geographic area in which entry via the Internet is permissible, you may, in lieu of submitting an entry on-line, enter by mail, by hand-printing your name, address, telephone number and contest number/name on an 8"x 11" plain piece of paper and telling us in 100 words or fewer "Where In The World Your Love Will Come Alive," and mailing via first-class mail to: Silhouette 20ᵗʰ Anniversary Contest, (in the U.S.) P.O. Box 9069, Buffalo, NY 14269-9069; (In Canada) P.O. Box 637, Fort Erie, Ontario, Canada L2A 5X3. Limit one 8"x 11" mailed entry per person, household and e-mail address per day. On-line and/or 8"x 11" mailed entries received from persons residing in geographic areas in which Internet entry is not permissible will be disqualified. No liability is assumed for lost, late, incomplete, inaccurate, nondelivered or misdirected mail, or misdirected e-mail, for technical, hardware or software failures of any kind, lost or unavailable network connection, or failed, incomplete, garbled or delayed computer transmission or any human error which may occur in the receipt or processing of the entries in the contest.

3. Essays will be judged by a panel of members of the Silhouette editorial and marketing staff based on the following criteria:

   Sincerity (believability, credibility)—50%
   Originality (freshness, creativity)—30%
   Aptness (appropriateness to contest ideas)—20%

   Purchase or acceptance of a product offer does not improve your chances of winning. In the event of a tie, duplicate prizes will be awarded.

4. All entries become the property of Harlequin Enterprises Ltd., and will not be returned. Winner will be determined no later than 10/31/00 and will be notified by mail. Grand Prize winner will be required to sign and return Affidavit of Eligibility within 15 days of receipt of notification. Noncompliance within the time period may result in disqualification and an alternative winner may be selected. All municipal, provincial, federal, state and local laws and regulations apply. Contest open only to residents of the U.S. and Canada who are 18 years of age or older, and is void wherever prohibited by law. Internet entry is restricted solely to residents of those geographical areas in which Internet entry is permissible. Employees of Torstar Corp., their affiliates, agents and members of their immediate families are not eligible. Taxes on the prizes are the sole responsibility of winners. Entry and acceptance of any prize offered constitutes permission to use winner's name, photograph or other likeness for the purposes of advertising, trade and promotion on behalf of Torstar Corp. without further compensation to the winner, unless prohibited by law. Torstar Corp and D.L. Blair, Inc., their parents, affiliates and subsidiaries, are not responsible for errors in printing or electronic presentation of contest or entries. In the event of printing or other errors which may result in unintended prize values or duplication of prizes, all affected contest materials or entries shall be null and void. If for any reason the Internet portion of the contest is not capable of running as planned, including infection by computer virus, bugs, tampering, unauthorized intervention, fraud, technical failures, or any other causes beyond the control of Torstar Corp. which corrupt or affect the administration, secrecy, fairness, integrity or proper conduct of the contest, Torstar Corp. reserves the right, at its sole discretion, to disqualify any individual who tampers with the entry process and to cancel, terminate, modify or suspend the contest or the Internet portion thereof. In the event of a dispute regarding an on-line entry, the entry will be deemed submitted by the authorized holder of the e-mail account submitted at the time of entry. Authorized account holder is defined as the natural person who is assigned to an e-mail address by an Internet access provider, on-line service provider or other organization that is responsible for arranging e-mail address for the domain associated with the submitted e-mail address.

5. Prizes: Grand Prize—a $10,000 vacation to anywhere in the world. Travelers (at least one must be 18 years of age or older) or parent or guardian if one traveler is a minor, must sign and return a Release of Liability prior to departure. Travel must be completed by December 31, 2001, and is subject to space and accommodations availability. Two hundred (200) Second Prizes—a two-book limited edition autographed collector set from one of the Silhouette Anniversary authors: Nora Roberts, Diana Palmer, Linda Howard or Annette Broadrick (value $10.00 each set). All prizes are valued in U.S. dollars.

6. For a list of winners (available after 10/31/00), send a self-addressed, stamped envelope to: Harlequin Silhouette 20ᵗʰ Anniversary Winners, P.O. Box 4200, Blair, NE 68009-4200.

Contest sponsored by Torstar Corp., P.O. Box 9042, Buffalo, NY 14269-9042.

PS20RULES

ENTER FOR A CHANCE TO WIN*

Silhouette's 20ᵗʰ Anniversary Contest

Tell Us Where in the World You Would Like *Your* Love To Come Alive... And We'll Send the Lucky Winner There!

Silhouette wants to take you wherever your happy ending can come true.

Here's how to enter: Tell us, in 100 words or less, where you want to go to make your love come alive!

In addition to the grand prize, there will be 200 runner-up prizes, collector's-edition book sets autographed by one of the Silhouette anniversary authors: **Nora Roberts, Diana Palmer, Linda Howard** or **Annette Broadrick**.

DON'T MISS YOUR CHANCE TO WIN! ENTER NOW! No Purchase Necessary

Silhouette®
Where love comes alive™

Visit Silhouette at www.eHarlequin.com to enter, starting this summer.

Name:

Address:

City: State/Province:

Zip/Postal Code:

Mail to Harlequin Books: **In the U.S.**: P.O. Box 9069, Buffalo, NY 14269-9069; **In Canada**: P.O. Box 637, Fort Erie, Ontario, L4A 5X3

*No purchase necessary—for contest details send a self-addressed stamped envelope to: Silhouette's 20ᵗʰ Anniversary Contest, P.O. Box 9069, Buffalo, NY, 14269-9069 (include contest name on self-addressed envelope). Residents of Washington and Vermont may omit postage. Open to Cdn. (excluding Quebec) and U.S. residents who are 18 or over. Void where prohibited. Contest ends August 31, 2000.   PS20CON_R2